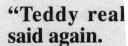 

"Teddy real... said again.

"Wonderful," West repeated. Leaning sideways and balancing on one arm, he met her lips in a kiss that took her by surprise, because she'd thought they were ending, not beginning.

Annie's skin began to tingle as West's lips lingered against hers. Her breath caught in her throat and her heart began a strange beat. All at once she was again remembering West's power, and wondered what it would be like to make love with him.

The kiss ended when Teddy twisted and held out his arms to West.

"Now he wants me," West groaned. "Story of my life. Nobody ever wants me until it's too late."

Annie's heart skipped a beat. She wished she could tell him how much she wanted him now, but she couldn't. He might think her desire meant she was willing to give up her dream for him, and how could she do that? The past few days with Teddy had fanned the spark into a full-blown fire again.

Dear Reader,

The other day, I was trying to figure out why I have always wanted to write romances—even before I ever read any. That choice came in my early teenage years while watching television Westerns, when I saw the dark, handsome and slightly vulnerable cowboys were never allowed to have a happily-ever-after with a woman. I, on the other hand, delighted in making sure they all ended up with the loves of their lives, on hundreds of sheets of notebook paper, in my own romances.

Now, thanks to you, the reader, I'm again playing matchmaker to my own lonely heroes and heroines—and loving it. Without meeting Gina in THE ONE-WEEK WIFE, how lonely Matt Gallagher would have ended up! And as for his brother, West—well, just turn the page and see what I have in store for him in THE ONE-WEEK BABY...

Hayley Gardner

THE ONE-WEEK BABY

BY

HAYLEY GARDNER

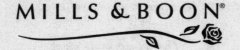

MILLS & BOON®

To Dan, as always, and happy sixteenth!
Special thanks to Melissa and Cris, whose suggestions
helped bring the Gallagher brothers to life.

*First published in Great Britain 2000
Harlequin Mills & Boon Limited,
Eton House, 18-24 Paradise Road, Richmond, Surrey TW9 1SR*

© Florence Moyer 1997

ISBN 0 263 81969 8

*Set in Times Roman 10½ on 12¼ pt.
01-0003-46310*

*Printed and bound in Spain
by Litografía Rosés, S.A., Barcelona*

1

Dear Mr. Gallagher,

Your book on getting what you want out of life was so awesome, I just had to go to your seminar. That's where you convinced me—I've got to run and lasso my dream while there's still time, just like you told us we should. You were so nice and caring about people's troubles during your class, I know you won't mind taking care of my Teddy while I'm gone. You shouldn't have a lick of trouble. I don't think I'll be gone past Saturday—at least, I hope not. Anyway, with you taking care of Teddy, I won't worry about a thing. I'll be in touch!

Thanks,
Marcia—the checker at the Shopette

P.S. I sent a copy of this note to my lawyer so she'll know my Teddy's in good hands.

Folding Marcia's note in two, West Gallagher gazed down at the blanket-covered, wicker laundry basket on his front porch. How nice, he thought uneasily, that Marcia-from-the-Shopette wasn't going to worry. He, on the other hand, had a feeling he was about to get plenty worried—unless, that was, by *Teddy* this Marcia was referring to her favorite stuffed animal.

But no… Something shifted under the blanket, and the surface rose and fell like an undulating wave. Whatever it was, it could move. Not a teddy bear then. Maybe a puppy.

Not a puppy. As West stood frozen in place on what had seconds before been his very boring front porch, he knew both guesses were wrong. He knew this because he thought this Marcia-from-the-Shopette would probably have taken a puppy or a stuffed bear with her while pursuing her dream. Only children ever seemed to prove a burden for parents when it came to moving on.

That he knew for a fact. Shortly after West had turned eight, his father had left home and not come back, and West distinctly recalled that neither he nor his eleven-year-old brother Matthew had been invited to join him. West knew now that either of them tagging along would have just slowed his father down. Marcia had probably left her very own version of a Pandora's box on his doorstep for the same reason— a child got in the way of personal freedom.

But his father had eventually returned, and West hoped now that just like Luke, Marcia would come back, too, full of remorse, maybe even in the week that she'd promised. West suddenly recalled himself as a little boy clinging to that exact same hope as days, and then weeks, went by without his seeing his old man, and then, when everything went out of control, his mother, and then his brother. Clenching his jaw, he forced back the memories. Just because he'd been left alone didn't mean that Marcia wouldn't return for her baby.

Did it?

His gut tightening, West looked up and down the street, hoping for a miracle. But then he heard a gurgling sound and looked down at the wicker basket illuminated in his golden porch light.

Blue elephants appliquéd on the blanket rose and fell, and West knew that no matter how much he wanted to remain in a pleasant, zombielike state of inactivity and denial, there *was* a baby under that cover, and he had to do something. But in that basket was a time bomb, just waiting for him to get close enough so it could explode and disintegrate his perfectly organized life, and he was very reluctant to unwrap the package.

The blanket's top edge suddenly flipped downward. A chubby baby, maybe six months old—and with what little he knew about babies, he was guessing—with a square face and wide mouth waved both hands at West, seemingly wanting to be picked up. A boy, from the looks of him.

"Marcia," West muttered under his breath, "even if you *were* feeling extremely grateful for my help, you should never have left me your firstborn son."

Damn, but he should have let well enough alone and remained a successful financial planner on the East coast. He should have ignored the burst of creativity that had led him to write his book on how he'd made something out of his life after his parents had given him up to the foster care system.

But, at the time, who would have guessed something like this could happen? Then all he'd known was that he wanted to pay tribute to one of his high school teachers, Joseph Hayden, who had taught him never to give up if he truly wanted something. There were too few people like Joe, liked and respected for helping others. West had always wanted to be one of them, helping people who'd been like him—floundering all alone in the world.

And from the looks of it, he thought wryly, staring down at the bundle of joy in front of him, that particular wish had just been granted.

He guessed he shouldn't complain too much. If he hadn't written his book, he wouldn't have been on television, and his father wouldn't have known how to contact him after twenty years of separation. Best of all, his father had known where his brother was, and West had been able to be the surprise best man at his brother's wedding. Up to now, seeing Matt so happy with his new wife, Gina, had been well worth the minor troubles that the fame from the book and seminars had brought him. Troubles like a slew of women sending him things—undies, nude photos…

And now a baby. What next? He frowned in alarm. Maybe he'd better cancel his upcoming infomercial. Someone might see it and leave him a wife!

The baby cooed and drew him out of his thoughts. "Uh, Teddy, I guess Mama's not coming back any second penitent and apologetic, huh?" Leaning down,

West picked up the child, deciding to stay outside to give Marcia a few more minutes to change her mind.

Once out of the basket, Teddy blew a bubble and arched back to look up at West. As heavily lashed, innocent brown eyes stared at him and the scent of baby lotion drifted up, something tugged inside West in the vicinity of his heart—which made him very nervous. He was getting too involved in this, just because the kid had reminded him of the past he didn't want to think about.

West sighed. Long ago in his first foster home, he'd learned that whining got you nowhere, but still, in this case, he figured maybe he was entitled to one little reversal in his otherwise upwardly mobile outlook on life.

"Why me?" he asked out loud.

The baby poked his finger into West's chin, reminding him who the important one was here.

"Yeah, yeah, Teddy, I know. The question is really why *you,* right? Let me tell you kid," he said in a low, man-to-man voice, "I've been there. My mother gave me away, too, so I can sympathize. Maybe you wound up in the right place with the right guy after all."

His eyes never shifting from West's, the kid seemed mesmerized. West wanted to think Teddy was agreeing, that he did feel better off here, but deep within, where West still felt the pain from his childhood, he knew better—kids needed their mothers.

"How could your mommy do this?" he asked Teddy, who finally blinked. At twenty-eight, West still hadn't figured out the answer to that. Each time he read or heard of someone abandoning their helpless child he got exasperated. In fact, he felt so strongly against children getting the kind of raw deal in life he had, he'd long ago vowed he'd never personally be responsible for putting any kid through the wringer of divorce or separation. Which meant, quite simply, he was never going to have kids.

That decided, there had never seemed to be any reason to get married. He wished the best for his brother and his new wife, of course, but from what West had observed around him, wedded bliss never lasted very long after the first couple of arguments. The only two relationships West had ever developed had ended swiftly when the ladies discovered they couldn't change his mind about having a family. So much for true love.

No kids, no marriage. He was not daddy material. He grinned at Teddy, awkwardly bouncing the baby in his arms. "Your mama certainly had me pegged all wrong, didn't she?"

Teddy ahhhed.

Well, the fact was, Marcia *had* lucked out. For no matter what his personal view was on having his own children, West couldn't stand the idea of actually turning the kid in to the authorities. His past in the foster care system had taught him officials tended to say one thing and do exactly another, and usually that other thing had nothing to do with what was good for the kid in question. Like the time they'd promised him he'd stay with his brother, then later dragged him away from Matt kicking and screaming, splitting them apart for twenty years. The hurt and mistrust from having gone through that still ran deep inside West and made him totally unwilling to call anyone for help now. Nobody was going to keep Teddy from eventually going home.

"We'll just have to find your mother, kid, and give you back," he said, awkwardly patting the baby's silky cheek. "I'll make sure she gets help first, though." He wasn't sure if he could make that happen, but Teddy gurgled and gazed up at him with trusting eyes that made him feel powerful.

If he had to blackmail Marcia into going for counseling, he would, West decided. He couldn't save all the kids in the world, but he for damned sure could help the one that had been dropped on his doorstep.

"Another minute or two, and we'll go in, okay?" West asked the baby, still hoping Marcia would reappear. To kill time, he gave Teddy a quick once-over to see what the baby might need immediately. Not food—Teddy was extremely content. Not diapers or a bath, either—he smelled baby-powder sweet. Good. That would buy him some time until he figured out what his next step would be.

"This could have been worse, kid." West chucked him gently under the chin. "At least you aren't old enough to remember being left behind by your mama."

Not like he'd been. He'd never forget. The day his mother had walked off and left him and Matt with the county, she'd worn a scalloped, white-lace collar and tiny pearl earrings, and her cheeks had been damp with tears against his when she'd hugged him goodbye. Then, her back straight, she'd turned and walked down the long hallway as the cavernous corridor echoed his crying, disappearing through the heavy front door of the building as the foster care people gripped his arms and waist to keep him from running after her.

Once in the system, all he'd had left was his brother Matthew. Within two weeks, the foster care people had split them up, too. A vacant sort of pain reminded West that he'd never lost his loneliness or his bitterness. Twenty years he'd spent with no real family, because foster care hadn't found a way to keep him and his brother together. Now, even though thanks to his father—or maybe thanks to his fame—he knew where his family was, they were all little more than strangers with a common beginning. His brother was busy in the air force, and his parents were back in Kentucky, together—for now, anyway…

Hell, no, West thought, boosting Teddy up against his shoulder. He wasn't about to trust the system to know what was best for any kid. He wasn't about to make Teddy go through what he had—years without anyone who cared about him in his life, too young and helpless to change things for himself. Adults had a choice. Kids didn't.

He glanced at Teddy. What the hell was he going to do with a baby? Babies needed things, like diapers, food….

It suddenly occurred to him that Marcia might have left either or both of those, or another note with whom to contact in case of an emergency on it—he should be so lucky—in the basket. With a rush of hope, holding Teddy securely with one arm, he knelt and started searching. He did find another blanket, a couple of disposable diapers, an empty bottle, and a piece of clothing that looked like long johns with feet—but no note.

"Looks like Mama didn't want to leave me an escape clause, huh, Teddy?"

Teddy suddenly let out a string of one-syllable sounds.

"Ha! I knew you were holding out on me," West said, grinning again, rising to his feet. "Since you do talk, maybe you can tell me why you're here. What lesson am I supposed to suffer through this time?"

The baby went serenely silent.

"Not squealing, huh? This is probably going to be one of those endure-till-you-get-things-right deals, isn't it?" No answer. "Okay, okay. I'll hold my questions until we find your mother. I can't wait to ask her a few. Like, on what page in my book did I offer to take in babies? And, what sort of bender was her common sense on when she equated anything I wrote with leaving you on a doorstep? But for now, it's time to go inside and spring into action."

First he'd check his seminar registration records for Marcia's address, then at the Shopette to see if they knew anything. But then again, maneuvering around the city with Teddy was going to be tricky without a car seat. Hiring a detective might be easier.

Trying to remember Marcia from the myriad faces he'd seen both at the Shopette and at his seminars, West set Teddy back down in the basket and grabbed both handles, preparing to carry the whole load over the threshold into his house. Before he got up, though, a car screeched to a stop in front of his house, and a woman shoved open the driver's side door.

"Please, wait!" she called over the top of her car. "I've got to talk to you!"

She was not Marcia-from-the-Shopette; West was certain he'd never seen this woman before. Straightening, he held either side of the basket as the slim woman hurried up the walk, her high heels clicking until she reached the wide circle of porch light.

"Uh, sorry, I can't talk," he said, avoiding the woman's eyes. "I've got laundry to finish."

"It's a good thing I'm here, then," she said, swinging her purse over her arm. "Don't you know you're supposed to take the baby out of his romper before you wash it?"

Ah, heck, now he had to look at her. "Are you sure?" He shot her a purposely incredulous look. "The kid made it through the spin cycle okay."

Pushing back a wispy gold tendril of hair that had strayed from her French twist, the woman rolled her eyes and shook her head. "Please tell me you aren't West Gallagher."

"Okay, I won't tell you that." Which was as good as admitting he was. Why on earth had he done that? Because the new arrival had on black, open-heeled sandals and nude hose, sophisticated with a hint of sexy? Because he was partial to honey-gold hair and big hazel eyes? Because he liked the black, body-skimming skirt she wore with that short jacket?

Hell, he was turning into an idiot over a pretty face. He had to start getting out more. "Who might you be, anyway?" West asked.

"Marcia Kinster's lawyer—Annie Robicheaux,'' she said, still looking frustrated. As if to prove it, she threw both hands up into the air, and West focused in on her nails. Shell pink. He loved pink on a female. Her lips were a glossy, almost natural peach—a very kissable color.

He scowled. Everything about this woman suited his tastes to perfection, except that she was a lawyer. It occurred to him that he ought to feel relieved. Here was someone watching out for Marcia's best interests. She could take Teddy off his hands. But still, she was a lawyer, and that made him hold his tongue for right now as he waited for the bomb to drop. He had no doubt that it would.

It was that kind of an evening.

He *was* West Gallagher. Annie Robicheaux stared at the tall, broad-shouldered man in front of her. According to Marcia Kinster, her client who had taken his seminar and was her reason for being here, Gallagher was a man with magnetism. Gallagher could mesmerize a crowd, make them remember their hurts, their pasts, and then convince them of how wonderful and powerful they all were despite everything. Gallagher could also make them think they actually had control over their futures. He could energize people with his stories and give them hope.

Her eyebrows rose incredulously. This guy? Impossible. Even though the man in front of her was attractive in a dark, steely eyed sort of way, and dressed in a ritzy shirt and nicely cut slacks, he seemed pretty mortal to her. But maybe that was because, made curious by Marcia Kinster's raves, she had read his book and had put what Gallagher did for a living on the same level as a hawker of cure-all tonic in the nineteenth century, selling an instant solution to your troubles. Chase your dream, change your life. How absurd.

Marcia had obviously gone off the deep end.

"It was bad enough that my client went to your silly seminar instead of paying my bill," she said, feeling the beginnings of a good tirade coming on— maybe one of her best. "But what on earth could she have been thinking of when she left her baby with you? Her child? With a dream chaser she doesn't really know?"

He glared at her wordlessly.

Annie shook her head sadly. Really, where was all his charisma? "I mean, I've read your book, and I must say I wasn't impressed. You seem to be living somewhere outside of reality."

"Actually, for tonight, I hope you're right," West said. "I hope this all turns out to be just one big, bad dream." He jiggled Teddy, who was beginning to squirm. "If you want a refund on the book, Ms. Robicheaux, I suggest you contact your bookstore. As it is, you've caught me in the middle of something important. So if you'll excuse me—"

"You don't seem to understand, Mr. Gallagher, so I'll make it clear," she said, her peach lips pursing. "I've come for the baby. Marcia has obviously made a horrible mistake."

"You're telling me," West said, shifting the

weight he was holding. Teddy found his rattle and began shaking it.

"Then you'll let me take Teddy?" she asked.

"Not on your life." He squinted his eyes at her. For all he knew, this lady was angry enough about Marcia leaving her baby with a "dream chaser" that she would turn Teddy right over to the foster care system if she got hold of him. "For some reason, I was the one she wrote the note to, authorizing me to take care of Teddy. Apparently, Marcia trusted me, but not anyone else." And neither should he.

Annie felt terrible. Marcia had called her twice yesterday, and she hadn't been able to return her calls. If she had and she'd learned what Marcia had been planning to do, she was certain she could have convinced the young woman to put her trust in *her,* and at the very least, she could have taken Teddy and avoided this whole scene. At best, she could have talked Marcia out of this fiasco.

This was all her fault. "I'm not just anyone. Teddy is my client."

"You don't say." West stared down at the top of the baby's head, his face serious. "Hey, Teddy, what do you pay your lawyer with—play money?"

"He uses charm and wit," she said, her lips wrinkling to show her disdain for his humor. "Two items you sorely lack."

"Yeah, well, it's easy to be cute when you're a baby. We older guys have to work at it." He grinned again.

Oh, good Lord, the man had a dimple. Annie decided it was time to get out of there before she discovered what else Gallagher had that made women like Marcia lose their better sense.

"Look, Marcia must have been hoping I'd come here and take Teddy. If not, why did she leave me these?" Yanking a second piece of paper out of her purse, Annie thrust it and the one she already held toward him. Putting down the basket, he took them, his large hand brushing against her fingers as he did so. A surprised look of mutual awareness lingered between them like fear after a lightning bolt.

She jerked her hand away and added, "I found them both when I got home. One's the note she left me with your address on it. How would she have gotten that, I wonder?"

"Off the checks I wrote at the Shopette, probably," West speculated. An argument for using cash if he ever heard one.

She didn't skip a beat. "There's also a copy of the letter she wrote you. If I hadn't been delayed at the office, I would have caught her in time to stop her from this ridiculous whim of hers to make her dream happen—whatever that dream might be."

"Why is it so ridiculous to want something wonderful to happen in your life?"

For a few seconds Annie stared into Gallagher's dark eyes. They held a warmth she wasn't used to seeing in the wealthy clients she'd been getting lately, and for a minute, she was caught in their comforting lock.

"I believe you shouldn't waste time hoping and planning for things that will never happen," she said, swallowing a tight throat. ''Dreams are a waste of valuable time.''

''I don't believe that. Dreams are all people really have to live for.''

''Marcia has her baby to live for, Gallagher. She didn't need to desert Teddy to go chasing rainbows. No dream is more important than a child's welfare.'' Her hazel eyes challenged him.

''I agree wholeheartedly.''

All of a sudden she was winning? She watched Gallagher read the letters she'd just handed him, uncertain she should be thinking in terms of winning and losing where he was concerned—it might be dangerous to assume anything so cut-and-dried about him. But she'd been thinking of her life and work in terms of winning and losing for a long time now, and it was hard to change. Back and forth, all day long, for the three years since she'd become a lawyer, and a few before that. Win—lose. Win a settlement. Lose a suit. Win a new client. Lose your dream…

She shook her head. A man like Gallagher would think in other terms, she knew. Such as dreaming and wishing, and that obstacles were imaginary images not to be conquered, but ignored. Well, she wasn't letting him ignore her.

Fully aware of the lawyer staring pensively at him, West finished the letters Annie had given him. One was a copy of the same one he had. The other, written on the same stationery in the same jagged handwriting, begged Annie Robicheaux to check on Teddy— just in case West Gallagher wasn't the paragon of virtue she'd assumed he was.

If Marcia hadn't been one-hundred percent positive about his character, why had she left Teddy with him? Women, West thought, made everything that should be easy very difficult. "Marcia should have just left her baby with you and not gotten me into this," he muttered, handing her back the notes and hoisting the basket and the baby back up.

"Exactly my point," she said.

"So why didn't she?"

Annie didn't know, but she could hazard a guess. Marcia Kinster had come to her law office desperate about the poor living conditions in her low-income apartment. Annie had promised to track down Marcia's absentee landlord and convince him to do needed repairs, but occupied with two cases for a couple of other clients who actually paid money, she hadn't had a chance to get to it yet. Maybe Marcia thought if she were too busy to handle all her work, then she would be too busy to help her out with Teddy.

And wasn't that a sad reflection on her? Because she was working hard to get wealthier clients so she could afford what she really wanted in life, she hadn't been there when Marcia had called yesterday. And being there for people who really needed her was why she'd become a lawyer.

"Whatever Marcia's reasons," West said when Annie didn't answer, "she went and involved me and my conscience. The only person I'm handing that baby over to is a member of its family."

Annie's eyes flashed fire. West was attracted by them for a minute, until he remembered that she'd scoffed about following one's dreams. Deflated, he reminded himself that he didn't have time in his life for a woman.

But that didn't mean he couldn't look.

"Be reasonable, Mr. Gallagher," Annie said softly. "I'm sure a man as busy as yourself doesn't have time for a baby. I do."

Her satiny tone annoyed West. She was as slick as the social workers who, just to shut him up, had kept promising him he would see his brother again soon. He'd had problems trusting people since. He wasn't about to turn Teddy over to Annie—whether she liked it or not. The powers that be had made Marcia-from-the-Shopette choose him to take care of her son, and he knew better than to tempt fate by saying no.

"Besides," Annie pushed when he seemed to be considering what she'd said, "why should you have to take care of a child who was dumped on you?"

"Because I want to," he said simply. "Aren't I novel?"

"You certainly are that," she replied with a sigh. "Men are always such a problem for me."

From fire to frustration. West had to grin. "So why are you so eager to take on Teddy yourself?" he asked.

She wasn't about to tell him the real reason, so she gave him the same excuse she was giving herself. "I don't feel right leaving him here with someone who is nothing more than a modern-day tonic salesman, pushing dreams instead of brown bottles. I'll bet you even have an infomercial."

"You have something against free enterprise?"

"You do have an infomercial!"

He didn't have time to answer. Teddy, who'd been playing with the sleeve of West's shirt up to that point, began to fuss and hold out his hands to Annie.

The empty feeling that had haunted Annie for years reached out and pulled at her again, but before she could reach for the baby, Gallagher put the basket down and picked Teddy up. Seeing the baby so close and longing to hold him herself frustrated her, so she pushed aside her feelings and resumed her argument—to win.

"Look, no matter why Marcia left Teddy with you," Annie said, "she abandoned her baby, which means she wasn't thinking too clearly—especially if she fell for your malarkey about being able to obtain your dreams simply because you want to."

He actually had the audacity to smile. "You think going after what you dream about is malarkey?" he asked. "Don't you have any fantasies you'd like to pursue?"

His midnight-blue eyes were just too darned deep, and for a few seconds Annie had a fantasy all right— a fantasy about Gallagher she had no right having in front of an innocent baby. She blinked it away. "I keep myself based in reality."

"What a shame." He looked regretful and, with his tousled dark hair and thick eyebrows over deep blue eyes, sexy, all at the same time.

All too aware she was staring, she couldn't take her eyes off the picture the man made with the baby. Gallagher was tall and broad-shouldered, a big, rugged man, yet he looked perfectly comfortable holding

Teddy. Teddy had no complaints, either, sucking on his fist as he leaned his head against Gallagher's chest. Her heart thumped and she wondered if maybe, just maybe, life was going to go her way for a change....

Stop it, Annie, she told herself. From the publicity she'd read about him, she and Gallagher were like oil and water. He drifted in a dreamworld while she toiled her tail end off in the real one.

"Really, Mr. Gallagher," she said, tired of arguing. Tired period. She'd had a long day with her clients, and now this. She wanted to get Teddy settled for the night at her place. "I'd hate to have to call in social services to make sure Teddy will be safe, but maybe that's what I should do."

"No," West protested, reaching out to catch her wrist in fingers of steel. Her eyes went frosty as she stared down at his hand. Almost immediately, his grip loosened.

"Listen, can we continue this discussion inside?" he asked. "I think he needs changing. Hang on a minute." With the baby balanced on his shoulder and secured with one arm, he moved over the basket and grabbed a diaper. "Would you mind toting the basket inside for me?"

"Mind? Mr. Gallagher, I have just begun to fight." She had absolutely no intention of going anywhere without Teddy, and the sooner she was able to convince him of that, the better.

2

Inside Gallagher's house, Annie's heels sank into thick, maroon carpeting as she followed West through the foyer into his living room. Putting the basket where he pointed on the floor at one end of the plush velvet sofa, she sat as West disappeared, diaper in hand and Teddy on his hip. Not for one second had he put the baby down, and it didn't look like he ever planned to.

"Fine, Gallagher," she muttered, staring at a glass cabinet containing expensive collector's cars, and then down at the gold watch on the carved-edge coffee table in front of her. "Trust me not to steal your valuables, but don't trust me not to steal someone else's baby."

How was she going to persuade Gallagher to give her Teddy so she could leave? She'd already played her ace threat—calling social services—and all it had gotten her was a few more minutes to change West's mind. Courtroom strategy would have her finding and taking advantage of his weak points to get Teddy, but time was working against her. And besides, from what she'd seen of West Gallagher so far, she had to wonder if he had any.

Closing her eyes briefly, Annie took a deep breath. She wasn't an ogre—not enough of one to call social services, anyway. But if for some reason Marcia didn't come back, neither she nor the man in the next room had any choice but to call in the authorities. Unlike West, she was a realist.

She hadn't always been that way. She'd been eighteen when she'd received her guardian's blessing to marry Jean-Pierre Robicheaux, a Cajun from outside New Orleans who'd swept her off her feet. She'd dreamed of her, Jean, and his three-year-old, motherless daughter, Mariette, being one happy family, with more children to come in the future. An only child, Annie had planned for at least three more of her own. But reality had proven very different from her dreams when Jean-Pierre had romanced his way out of her life and into someone else's.

As if Jean's cheating and desertion hadn't been bad enough, she'd lost Mariette, too. She'd made the mistake of thinking of the little girl as her own child, especially after Mariette had started calling her Mommy. The moment Jean had driven away with his daughter waving goodbye to her, Annie's heart had broken.

Her throat tightened. It was at that moment her wish to have her own child had taken root deep inside her. Over the years the idea had budded and blossomed into a full-grown desire that she'd tucked away near her heart, where she rarely probed, ready to be felt again when the time was right. To have her own child and be loved like Mariette had loved her again—unconditionally—was her dream.

Annie swallowed the lump in her throat and jumped out of her seat, pacing the room. She was nowhere near having her own child. Working as hard as she had lately to build up her practice, she'd had no time for relationships—and a baby had to have a father. Physically, the only eligible man she'd come across in weeks was Gallagher, and he floated around like a carefree butterfly with all his talk of dreams. She'd dealt with plenty of dreamers in her family; she hardly needed to net herself this one.

Gallagher's loud groan interrupted Annie's thoughts. She didn't exactly know where he was, so she stood where she was in the living room and called, "Having trouble, Gallagher?"

"Nothing I can't handle," he yelled. After a brief hesitation he added, "I stuck myself with a pin."

A pin? "Gallagher, that was a disposable diaper. They don't need pins."

"Now you tell me."

Her eyes narrowed. She thought he might be teasing her, but in case it turned out he wasn't, she added his lack of knowledge about children to the argument against his keeping Teddy, which she was going to start the second he returned to the room—assuming he was planning to, that was.

This was such a time waster! Frustrated, she started pacing again. If she'd been there for Marcia, then her client would have come to her for help with Teddy, and she wouldn't be going through this now. In the first months of her practice, Annie had made it a point to be there for all her clients, even though most couldn't pay her. Divorcing Jean-Pierre had been the reason.

She'd been like Marcia during the proceedings—young, without money, and needing someone to help her. Because her low-cost legal aid had not been top quality, she'd ended up having to pay Jean-Pierre alimony for cheating on her. The extreme unfairness was why she'd worked so hard to become a lawyer, so people who were working-class and needy like she'd been would have some place to go when someone took advantage of them. She'd believed in what she wanted to do so much that she'd turned down invitations to join firms that took very few pro bono cases, and then only high-profile ones. The very thought of working for such firms had made her sick. So she'd set up her own law practice and went about trying to achieve her dreams. She could have it all, she thought. A profession she loved, and someday her baby.

She'd been wrong.

In the beginning she'd taken on mostly indigent clients. As her reputation for winning tough cases grew, more paying clients sought her out, and she'd stopped having to worry about paying her bills every month. That had been nice—too nice. She'd started saving for expanding her office and for her baby-to-be. Unfortunately, the more time the paying clients demanded, the more she'd had to let her pro bono cases slip. In working toward her dream of having a baby, she'd forgotten what was important—people like Marcia and Teddy.

And that was why she wanted Teddy.

Plopping back down on the couch and leaning over, she picked up Gallagher's gold watch and studied its gleaming beauty. West's reported charisma enabled him to convince people to hand over their hard-earned cash in exchange for listening to his blarney, and he bought gold watches and toy cars. What a waste compared to what she wanted money for. She wished she could understand why all her education and hard work couldn't get her the money his ideas, sparkle and gift of gab did. Life was so perversely lopsided sometimes.

"You aren't thinking of running off with that, are you?" Gallagher came through the doorway, Teddy snuggling against his broad shoulder.

He shouldn't tempt her, Annie thought—she still had her electric bill to pay. "No," she said, putting it back. "I was just thinking how strange it is you trust me with your valuables, but not with Teddy."

"The watch can be replaced. Kids can't." She heard the warning behind his lightly stated words. He felt a responsibility toward Teddy, too, he seemed to be saying, and he was ready for a battle. Well, that was fine with her. She'd failed Marcia once. This time she was going to remember why she'd become a lawyer. This time she was coming through for her client.

Gallagher shifted Teddy and rearranged the towel covering his shoulder and his jet black cotton shirt. Her eyes narrowed. That was *not* the shirt he'd had on when he'd left the room. And his hair was wet along his forehead, and his mouth was twisting as if he'd just sucked on a lemon—or as if he'd tasted something detestable while he'd been changing diapers.

All of a sudden, despite the seriousness of the situation, she began to laugh. "He christened you, didn't he?"

"I have no idea what you are talking about," Gallagher said. He looked down at Teddy. "When did you teach the lady baby babble, Ted?"

"C'mon, Mr. Gallagher, when you groaned, don't think for one minute I fell for that pin story. You were changing diapers, and the little guy squirted you. I'm sure you didn't even see it coming—especially not after it hit you in the eyes." She licked her lips to keep from laughing and sat down.

Gallagher's mouth twisted as though he were trying not to smile. "You can try humor to persuade me if you want, but what it all boils down to, Ms. Robicheaux, is that I consider the matter of Teddy settled." His midnight-blue eyes spoke volumes as he walked toward the couch and came to a stop in front of her. "I'm keeping the baby, and I need to know what I have to do to get you out of my life."

"You say that now," Annie said, "but what are you going to do if Teddy wakes up in the middle of the night crying? Or suddenly develops a bad diaper rash? Or can't keep down a bottle of milk?"

West remembered he was arguing with a pro, which was bad, considering he wasn't at all certain of his own skill in taking care of Teddy. Sitting, trying not to let a surge of anxiety show on his face, he plopped the baby down on the couch between him and Annie, keeping one hand near Teddy's shoulder in case he made any sudden moves. What *would* he do if something really bad happened? He'd barely gotten through the diaper change.

West gazed speculatively at Annie. If only he weren't so worried she would turn the kid over to foster care as soon as she got her shell-pink-tipped fingers on him, he'd give the baby to her and save himself a lot of trouble. But heck, what was he worried about? Convincing people how they should be thinking was his business. He'd have to hang it up if he couldn't convince Annie Robicheaux he had Daddy of the Year potential.

"If any of those things happen to Teddy," he said carefully, "I'll do the same thing you would do." What that was, he didn't know. He'd taken care of his share of babies for the Drews, his foster parents for about a year, but that had been fourteen years ago... What did new parents do?

Books. There had to be books on taking care of Junior.

Even though Gallagher kept one hand resting on Teddy, having a baby near the edge of the sofa made Annie nervous. Wanting a barrier to prevent Teddy from taking an accidental dive off the sofa, she looked around.

She found her solution in a straight-backed chair in the adjoining room and, rising, she went for it. Pushing the coffee table out of the way, she pulled the chair up to form a fence.

"There. That's better, isn't it, West?" She raised her lashes and all he saw were her eyes. He got the intense feeling he was being sucked into one of those bottomless black holes—only this one was hazel.

"I can call you West, can't I?" she asked.

"No. Teddy was fine without the chair. I'm watching him."

"Human beings are fallible, *West.*"

"Tell me about it," he agreed, eyeing her as she took a long, slim pillow and placed it between the chair and the baby. "Some are even paranoid." And controlling.

"Cautious." She sat. "Accidents happen. Marcia told me Teddy's six months old. He can roll over, but he's just learning to sit up. Did you know that?"

"Of course not. How would I know that?"

"Exactly."

"Look, Annie—I can call you Annie, can't I?"

"No."

He grinned. "You have no idea how pleasant a diversion you've been, but I think it's time you went home."

"The baby," she said through gritted teeth, her patience strained. "I cannot believe you are actually considering keeping him. How are you going to handle this? Teddy is going to need full-time care, supplies, formula, and a whole bunch of other things."

"I know what a baby needs," West told her, reaching over to pat Teddy's stomach absently. "He needs his mother. You're Marcia's lawyer. Do you have any idea where she might have gone?"

Annie barely heard his question. Her gaze lingered on the width of Gallagher's hand, and on how long his fingers were. Feeling her heart throbbing against her ribs, she swallowed nervously. She couldn't be attracted to a dream chaser—couldn't afford the mental anguish that could only come of it, and she dang well knew it. She had to win her point and get Teddy out of here.

"Annie?" he prompted. "Teddy's mother?"

"I can't tell you anything." She did have Marcia's address, but she couldn't tell him without breaking Marcia's lawyer-client confidence. She'd call as soon as West let her leave with Teddy, but she had a feeling Marcia wouldn't leave her baby with someone only to go back to her own place. What would be the point?

From somewhere a clock chimed nine, and Annie bristled. Having worked a full twelve-hour day before she'd gone home and found the notes, she wished now only to take Teddy back to her apartment and curl up with him on her bed. How much longer was Gallagher going to let this go on?

"Look, West, this isn't a lark. There's no one to help you when Teddy starts acting like a real baby instead of a cute television ad. I've seen the publicity promos on your seminar. You're a bachelor—"

"Good thing, too. I'd hate having to explain you and Teddy to a wife." His gaze swept over her with great appreciation and mild amusement. If he weren't so irritated with the entire situation, he might have asked her out. But things as they were…

"Try to pay attention now, West," she said sternly. "You have to work—"

"So do you."

"But I'm a woman," she said from between gritted

teeth. "Women know the differences between a baby's cries. We know the words to say when they're sick. We have instincts where babies are concerned."

"You don't have to tell me about females," he said agreeably. His grin was friendly, open and sexy, all at the same time. "I know all about them. They're cuddly and soft. They turn to men when they're lonely and afraid, and when they want to be comforted and held."

Annie's eyes took in Gallagher's muscular arms and her stomach fluttered. It had been so long since she'd turned to a man for anything. Curling up in West's arms right now and letting him just hold her would be so nice....

She clenched her fingernails into her palms to get a grip on herself. What was she thinking?

"Speaking of holding," West added, "I can cuddle real well. I've never had any complaints from any babies." He met her eyes, his own still twinkling. "Or from women, either."

Her head cocking, she flashed her eyes at him. "Do you have an answer for everything?"

"No." West glanced down at the baby, regret falling over his rugged features. "I don't have an answer for why some people go off and leave their innocent kids behind. I don't have any idea of what to do about the problem, either. All I know is that for some reason, I was given Teddy here to take care of." He gazed up at her. "And I know I can't test fate by letting him go until Marcia comes. You do believe in fate, don't you, Annie? That maybe we were all brought together here tonight to learn something about ourselves?''

His voice and his eyes swept over her now, imploring her to understand his feelings, drawing her in, and she watched him for a full minute, caught up in the spell his warm voice was weaving over her. A man like West who could feel so deeply would never allow Teddy to come to any harm. Maybe she ought to leave the baby here. What could it hurt?

"Go home, get some rest," he urged in a low, soothing voice, echoing her own thoughts. "You can trust me, Annie. I'm not just a dream chaser." His almost hypnotic, blue-eyed gaze lowered to look at Teddy.

Was he aware, Annie wondered, that whenever he watched Teddy, his normally empty eyes softened and warmed to an intensity that made her shiver? Marcia was right. West Gallagher was a spell weaver who could make you believe in him with all your heart....

Charisma! Annie jerked up straight. That damned charisma! "You're trying to talk me into leaving," she said.

"It almost worked, too, didn't it?"

Rising from the sofa, Annie strode across the room and back, furious. She *had* almost fallen under his spell. No wonder West was so popular on the lecture circuit. He was a *master* at manipulation. Her ex could take lessons from him!

"But it didn't work, West. I'm not going anywhere until you agree to give me Teddy! You won't be able to take care of him as well as I can."

"Why? Because you're a woman and I'm a man?"

Teddy gave a gentle cry, and Gallagher reached down to pick him up. The child was all baby blue against the shoulder of the big man's black shirt as Gallagher gently rocked him. "Be my guest and stick around a while longer. See how good a parent a man can be."

He wanted her to stay longer? Annie changed direction abruptly. "Even allowing you your point— that a man can be a good parent—a woman is always better. Basic instinct. I'd definitely be a better parent than you."

"I'll bet you're wrong," he said.

She stopped short. Always a quick thinker, she could immediately see the usefulness of what to him was probably only an offhand, meaningless utterance.

"You're on," she said before she could consider the ramifications and change her mind. "I'll take that bet. Monday's the Fourth of July—a federal holiday. Courts are closed. So I'll bet you by Monday evening, I'll have proven to you how much more Teddy prefers a female to a male taking care of him, so well that you'll let me take Teddy home and promise to forget about the two of us. If you aren't absolutely convinced, I'll leave the care of him to you and go graciously."

Even though she offered the last, she had no intention of leaving Teddy here with him at all. She didn't trust Gallagher to care for the child correctly for even a week. Marcia had obviously only brought her son here because she felt she had nowhere else to turn. But she'd reached out once more with her notes to Annie, and Annie believed the woman wouldn't have done that if she hadn't harbored a hope that her lawyer would come get her son.

Annie took a deep breath of determination. She'd failed Marcia once by not being there for her. She wasn't about to fail her twice.

What a royal pain the lady lawyer had turned out to be. West sat where he was, trying not to eye her long legs at the same time he considered her challenge. He thought he was good at maneuvering people, but Annie was a pro. He wanted to throw her out, but he had a feeling that would only compound his problems. If she went straight to social services, Teddy would no doubt be in foster care by midnight.

But his compassion wasn't the only reason he couldn't hand Teddy over to her. By producing a book enticing people to run after their dreams, he'd inadvertently gotten Marcia to run away from her responsibility. He figured he owed it to the clerk to take care of her kid for at least a few days and give her the chance to come to her senses.

Then there was the fact that Annie was a lawyer. Even if he gave Teddy to her, she might be ethically bound to call the police anyway after a couple days and tell them everything. Not only would Teddy wind up in foster care, West himself would have to explain to authorities why some strange woman had left a baby on his doorstep. How could he explain something he didn't understand himself?

Even if he could pull that off, he doubted they'd be pleased he hadn't called the police immediately to report the abandoned baby. It would make him look suspicious as hell. And if the story leaked to the papers... He'd made it big motivating people, and he didn't want those same people to think he might be guilty of something and as a result feel like they'd been made fools of for believing in him. He also didn't want to lose his work. It was all he had.

And finally—he *was* worried about taking care of Teddy by himself. The baby would have to have things, starting tonight, and West didn't know if he could pull this off alone. What if the kid got sick in the next few days before his mother came back? He'd *need* Annie's help.

So, damn it all, the bet she'd offered might be the answer to all his immediate problems. Let her think what she wanted about Monday night. Teddy wasn't going anywhere. He couldn't afford to give her the baby any more than he could chance letting her loose tonight without Teddy.

"Okay," he said. "You can stay."

"You didn't have a choice."

He grinned. "Didn't I? Try to remember, I'm bigger than you."

"Bully."

"You never let anyone get the last word, do you?"

"No," she said, shaking her head. "They teach us that in law school." Her eyes glinted with satisfaction.

West wished he felt as happy as she looked. Three days with Annie and a baby. He groaned inwardly, picturing the carefully maintained control he'd had over his life flying out of his hands and away on a flying carpet—no, make that on a large flying diaper, with a fat, laughing baby on the ground waving a magic wand, keeping it above West's head, just out of his reach. Staring down at Teddy, he blinked away the image. Ridiculous. One lone six-month-old baby couldn't possibly change his whole life.

He gazed up at Annie. Maybe not, but a grown woman could. He'd have to be on his guard—starting now.

3

Unable to convince Gallagher to let her watch Teddy while *he* went to the store for supplies, Annie had driven to the Shopette after he'd argued, successfully, that with no car seat, they couldn't both go and take the baby. That would be putting Teddy in jeopardy—and, he'd said with that know-it-all smirk on his face, breaking the law.

"Of course you wouldn't want to do that," Annie said out loud, mocking only herself as she drove away from Marcia's apartment building. The manager had said she'd gone on vacation—which was good, because it implied she'd be coming back. He did not, however, know where she'd gone.

Now Annie headed toward her own apartment to get some clothes. It was understood, at least she hoped, that she'd be staying at West's house during this bet of theirs. She knew he'd let her back inside. She had the diapers and formula, and by the time she returned, he was bound to be desperate.

In a way, she was pleased *she'd* been the one to go, because the trip had given her the opportunity to speak with the clerks who worked with Marcia at the

Shopette, a large supermarket halfway between her home and Gallagher's. Telling them she was Marcia's lawyer, Annie had learned Marcia had quit her job the day before, and no one knew what her plans were.

That, Annie guessed, put her one up on West Gallagher. Knowledge was power. She believed that so much she had also bought a how-to book on babies, just in case there was something she'd forgotten since she'd stopped baby-sitting her neighbors' babies when she'd opened her law office. She was determined to care for Teddy to the extent that he would start smiling the second she walked into a room.

At home, Annie quickly changed into jeans and a T-shirt and packed a small bag, but then she stood at her door and thought about what she was about to do. Really thought. West Gallagher was a total stranger, and she was going to move in with him for three days. Three days—and nights. She didn't care if he did have broad shoulders, blue eyes, and infinite compassion for abandoned babies. Now that she was due to head back to his house, she felt like she was playing a role in a survival movie for women, and the narrator was telling the viewers, "Under no circumstances do what Annie Robicheaux is about to do."

What she needed was some assurance that she'd be safe. She thought guns were a scourge on the earth, was too afraid pepper spray would be turned against her, and had two left feet when it came to all those defensive moves they taught women—as if she really believed she, at five foot three, one hundred and ten pounds, could flip a six-foot, two-hundred-pound West Gallagher on his butt anyway. No, what she needed was some real protection—the kind that would totally overwhelm West Gallagher if he chose to get funny on her while they were wrestling over Teddy.

She needed her aunt Gigi.

It was close to ten-thirty when Annie made the turn onto Gallagher's street. Before leaving her apartment, she'd left a message on her aunt's machine, telling the older woman that she was moving in with a strange man over the weekend, the address, and not to worry. That was sure to get her aunt here in an eye blink.

She smiled fondly at the thought of Gigi Perkins, the only parent she'd known since her own had given her up. Growing up with Aunt Gigi had been a bit like a walk on the wild side of life, and except for Jean-Pierre, Annie had strayed in the direction of establishment just to cope with her aunt's eccentricities.

Annie smiled again as she pulled into Gallagher's driveway and followed it to where it swung into an open garage under his house. If her message shocked Gigi, it would serve her right for going on that Caribbean cruise with the mailman the year before without any warning, and calling Annie an old lady because she'd been upset.

Gigi's car wasn't there yet, but Annie knew she'd come as soon as she got the message. Her aunt had never failed her—unlike almost everyone else in her life.

Pushing aside bad thoughts, she parked and got out, pulling her purse strap over her shoulder and patting the baby manual inside. Her security blanket. She wasn't about to rely on only a rusty memory and her own judgment when it came to taking care of another human being—especially one who couldn't talk yet.

Grabbing two of the four sacks from the market, she walked around to the front of the house because the kitchen entrance was locked and she didn't want to ring the bell in case she woke up Teddy. At the doorway of the living room, she stopped when she saw Gallagher.

He was on the far side of the couch, holding Teddy, his cheek resting on the baby's head. Annie's breath caught. The man really seemed to care about what happened to this child. She stared, unable to move, but then she warned herself not to make too much of what she was seeing. West was just keeping Teddy entertained, that was all. She would have done exactly the same thing. He hadn't rounded the curve and sur-passed her in this parenting game. She'd have her chances to prove herself better, and then she would get out of there and away from West Gallagher.

And while she was here, she didn't have to think about the fact that West was a man if she didn't want to. Just plain getting by in this world was hard enough without her remembering she was a woman with needs, too.

"I'm back," she called in a whisper, just in case Teddy was sleeping.

He wasn't, she saw when Teddy raised one of his small hands in the air as though he thought the fem-inine voice might be his mother. He looked confused for a second, and gave a short wail.

West cooed in the baby's ear to distract him, welcoming the chance to hide the relief on his face that Annie had returned. Not because she was a welcome sight and easy on his eyes, but because she'd brought formula.

That's what he told himself.

"Did you get everything?" he asked her.

"Everything I put on *my* list," she said. He smiled, and she wondered if her point had even registered.

"I think he's cutting teeth. Did you think of a teething ring?"

"Standard equipment," she said, as if she knew exactly what a thoroughly modern baby needed. Actually, she had just walked up and down the baby aisle, snatching whatever looked necessary—and that had been about one of everything. Then she'd taken a quick peek in the baby manual and found out that six-month-olds could eat baby oatmeal and pureed fruit, and were supposed to be starting on chunky foods, so she grabbed boxes and jars, too.

"If you'll just show me where your kitchen is, we can get this stuff unpacked and a bottle prepared. Teddy has to be getting hungry."

"True." He carried the baby toward the far side of the room and led her through another door into a shining, utilitarian kitchen, unlocking the rear entry at her request. Hurrying outside, Annie got the other two sacks, leaving her overnight bag in the car for now. Feeding Teddy came first—then they would discuss sleeping arrangements. Back inside the kitchen, she started unbagging the groceries, taking a second to steal a look at West and wonder if he slept in the buff.

Get in, get out, Annie, she reminded herself, blushing as she ripped the plastic packaging off a refrigerator magnet shaped like a baby's bottle. With resolve, she plopped it on the face of the refrigerator to hold the schedule she was going to make later.

Caught by surprise, feeling as though his territory was being invaded, West stared at the magnet on his refrigerator door. If he'd seen anything like that before, it hadn't been something he'd paid any attention to. Why Annie needed a magnet, he had no idea, but he had a question. "I don't suppose you could have gotten a regular old black magnet?"

"Like in science class?" Teasing him because he looked so serious, she shuddered dramatically, a grimace on her delicate features, and shook her head.

"I didn't think so." He sighed.

"Is something wrong?"

"It's so…" At a loss for words, he shrugged.

"Precious?" She smiled. "Don't worry, Gallagher, a preference for cuteness isn't catching. In a couple of days Teddy and I will be gone, and we'll take all signs of adorable with us."

"Teddy will be gone *if* and only if you win the bet," West reminded her, rearranging the baby in his arms. "Which reminds me. How are we going to judge who's better with Teddy?"

"I've been thinking about that. Each time one of us comes up with something that needs to be done for Teddy, he or she will get a point, and the totals will be the final determining factor—assuming Teddy likes us equally.'' She smiled. ''But don't worry, that will never happen.'' She took out the teething ring and gave it to him.

''That's right, it won't.'' Very carefully, he ripped off the cardboard package without reading it, and stuck it in the freezer.

''Why are you doing that?'' she asked.

''Common sense. Cold numbs pain.'' He raised his thick dark eyebrows. ''Point one for me.''

Annie shook her head. ''Point one for both of us. Wash anything new out of a package before you let a baby put it in his mouth.''

Teddy still in his arms, West rose to pull the ring back out of the freezer and go to the sink.

''Look, West, Teddy needs a bottle,'' Annie said, ''and I can't get to it until you're done with the water, so why don't you put him in his basket or let me hold him for you?''

''Yeah, sure,'' he said, his guard going up. ''You'll hold him all the way to your car, right?''

''I'm not going to run off with him. I promise,'' she said. ''Trust me.''

''I trust nobody,'' he replied, holding Teddy with his left arm. His right hand did two jobs at once as he ran the hot water and held the teething ring.

''You must trust me a little bit, or I wouldn't be here with you.''

''You're here just because I don't trust you,'' West admitted, purposely not looking over at Annie. He didn't want to see if his remark had hurt her feelings. He didn't want to know what she was thinking, and he didn't want to have already noticed she'd changed clothes while she'd been out, or that her T-shirt and jeans were almost as sexy as the short skirt and V-neck blouse had been earlier. This whole arrangement was unsettling as hell, and he wanted to pretend Annie wasn't there—but he couldn't.

But she had come back, alone, and he supposed that he could try a little harder than he was. Besides, doing anything with a baby in one arm was more difficult than he'd imagined it could be. He sighed. "Okay, I give in. Please hold him for me."

"It's a good thing judges aren't as hard to convince as you are—I'd never win a case." She cooed to the fussing baby as she took him from West. Teddy curved into her body as though they were meant for each other and laid his head against her breast and her swiftly beating heart.

As he quickly washed the ring and then put away the rest of their supplies, West watched Annie's every move out of the corner of his eye in case she started toward the door with Teddy. But she just stood where she was, holding the baby with a strange look on her face. West almost asked her what was wrong, but some inner sense of self-preservation screamed at him not to, that he'd be sorry if he started caring enough about her to ask, so he didn't.

After he got the basket to put the baby in—a compromise so that neither of them would be in total control of Teddy—Annie, back to normal, made a score sheet to keep track of their points and put it under the magnet on the fridge. Then she filled his sink and washed the new bottles in hot, soapy water.

"So how come you're not married?" she asked to make conversation.

He froze. Literally, while he was opening up a jar of baby food, he stiffened as though he'd been blocked in dry ice.

"Not that it's really your business," he said conversationally as he recovered and set about feeding Teddy. "But I've been too busy following my dream to deal with marriage. No wife and kiddies for me."

"No family ever?" The second after the words came out, Annie winced. Really, why was she asking Gallagher questions about himself? She was simply not that interested in the man.

"Ever," he agreed lightly.

"I think it would be pure misery to live life alone."

"You get used to it," he said, but to Annie the words sounded forced, and she wondered if he had.

"I never will." Annie was at a bad angle at the sink, so she couldn't read his eyes to see if they reflected the same level of nonchalance as his voice. So instead, she took in what she could see of him, his thick, dark brown lashes and the shadowy stubble of a beard on his cheeks. He was a mystery. He surrounded himself with people he tried to help during his seminars, yet he wanted no family.

"So what is this dream you've been chasing?" she asked, opening a can of formula.

"Two dreams." He tilted the spoon and got most of the applesauce in Teddy's mouth. "Renovating this house and obtaining total control over my life."

"Good luck on the last. Take it from me, no one ever has total control over his life. There are always outside factors entering into it—other people's wishes, friends and family you care about…'' Her voice drifted off as she saw a pained look come over his face. ''Is that why you don't want a wife and children, West? Because they would interfere with what you want to do?''

West gazed at her intently. ''I think Teddy would really like a bottle soon.''

''No problem,'' she said sweetly as she finished readying Teddy's bottle. Realizing that since he'd changed the subject from personal back to Teddy, he obviously wanted to keep their relationship superficial, she thought that would be fine with her.

The doorbell rang, and she remembered she forgot to tell him something.

''Uh, Gallagher?''

Rising, he thrust Teddy into her arms. ''Clean him up, would you? That can only be Marcia, having realized the error of her ways.''

''Uh, I don't think so—''

''It's either her,'' he said, already headed out of the kitchen to the hall, ''or another baby on my doorstep.''

Another baby? ''How many single mothers do you know, anyway?'' she called after him. But she didn't have time to speculate as she wiped Teddy's mouth and cheeks and slipped the bottle into his mouth.

West, hurrying to the door, thought it was just as well Marcia had returned. He didn't know how he would have survived with Annie in the house until Monday night. It was bad enough they obviously couldn't relate to each other—and the questions she was asking were unnerving—he was also so damned attracted to her he couldn't think straight. He usually believed nothing in his life ever happened without a reason, but why his path had ever crossed with Annie's he had absolutely no idea in the world....

"Marcia, thank God you're back!" he said as he flung open the door. But instead of a familiar face, he saw an older woman he didn't know holding her arms straight out in front of her. She had long, layered hair that fell down past her shoulders and she wore a flowing, jewel blue silk dress. Somehow she appeared oddly familiar, although West was positive they'd never met.

Suddenly he knew—just sensed somehow—that Annie was behind him. Turning slightly, he saw he was correct. She was holding Teddy, and smiling at the newcomer. Uh-oh. Trouble.

"Oh, you poor little *babeee!*" the older woman cried. "I am sick over this! I am taking you right home with me."

Scowling, afraid she was going to grab Teddy, West moved to stand in front of Annie and Teddy to protect the baby from the stranger with the suspiciously fake French accent crossing the threshold. Another woman showing up to claim the child? This was too much to handle for one evening.

"Look, lady, I don't know who you think you are," he said when the newcomer stopped directly in front of him, "and I don't know why I've suddenly become so popular, but you can't come in, and you definitely can't have Teddy—"

"It's okay, Aunt Gigi. You're already in, and West doesn't bite once he warms up."

Casting him a scornful look and tossing back her masses of auburn hair, "Aunt Gigi" swept around West and went right to Annie, hugging the smaller, younger woman to her more than ample bosom as well as she could with the baby between them. "*Ma petite,* my sweet child, you have flipped your noodle right to the ceiling, and it is sticking there. How can you move in with a man you barely know?"

"It was easy," West said, relieved that Annie, not Teddy, was the *babeee* in question. "Your niece just showed up on my doorstep and announced she was staying. I took her right in. All she was missing was a basket and a few of her marbles. But the baby brought a basket with him, so maybe she's planning on sharing. I guess her marbles will have to stay missing."

"Gallagher, if you want funny, hire a comic, okay?" Annie suggested, shaking her head at him. "Aunt Gigi, this is West Gallagher. West, Gigi Perkins."

Gigi clasped her hands to her chest and ignored the introduction. The older woman was very flamboyant compared to Annie, who was classy no matter what she wore, but yes, West could see the resemblance.

"You weren't going to warn me we were having a houseguest, dear?" West asked Annie.

"Well, I was," she said, turning pink in the cheeks, honestly embarrassed. It was *his* house, and he had every right to be annoyed. "But we got sidetracked with our conversation."

About babies and families. West stared at Annie
for a long minute. For a man who'd been avoiding
the first and living without the last for years, all of a
sudden he had more people in his life than he knew
what to do with. Teddy, Marcia, Annie, and now Aunt
Gigi. And he didn't like it. Unfortunately, he had no
idea what to do to get rid of everyone, except to give
Teddy to Annie and let her leave.

He couldn't do that. He couldn't abandon Teddy.
The memory of how he felt when he'd been a young
boy and totally alone was just too clear to him, and
he had an emotional stake in the baby's life now. In
short, whether he liked it or not, he was stuck with
all of them for a while. He glanced at the three and
his gaze rested on Aunt Gigi. "I suppose you want
to move in here, too," West said dryly.

"Au contraire!" Gigi swung around to face her
niece. "I have been agonizing about this ever since
you called, Annie. This is a horrible thing you've
done, moving in with this man. He could be anyone.
He could be a bigamist!"

"Hey, wait just a minute—" West protested, but
Annie was answering her aunt as though he weren't
even there.

"No way, Aunt Gigi. West has these *dreams* he's
chasing after. He's too busy working on them to have
one wife, let alone two or three."

"He's not a seducer of innocent women?" Gigi
asked, a hint of disappointment in her voice.

West grinned and said saucily, "Sure I am. The
line starts at the door."

"We-est!" Annie groaned. "Don't encourage her."

"But I have to," he said, grinning because this whole situation was starting to seem awfully funny—absurd even. And he was starting to feel a bit reckless. "If I don't encourage her, who will? I make a living helping people achieve their dreams, remember? If your aunt's dream is to meet up with a seducer of innocent women, who am I to object? I'll be happy to play the part if she wants."

For a few seconds, merriment exploded in Annie's eyes like an old-time flashbulb, and West could have sworn she wanted to laugh, but then she seemed to sober up and become perfectly serious again.

"He's kidding, Aunt Gigi. My virtue is safe," Annie said, although West noted she sounded far from certain about that. "Tell her, West."

"Of course I'm kidding. Her virtue is safe," West told Gigi.

"Then I must ask…" Gigi said to Annie with an airy sweep of her hand. "If he does not want a wife, and he does not want anything else, why on earth are you wasting time with him?"

4

"Teddy," Annie and West explained simultaneously, and West pointed to the baby in Annie's arms.

"Oh, no!" Gigi's mouth pursed. "You mean you've had a babeee—with him?" Staring at West, her eyes widened with disbelief. "Why on earth would you do that?"

"Hey, what's wrong with me?" West asked.

"I'm sure she didn't mean it the way it sounded," Annie soothed, the corners of her mouth turned upward in a semblance of a smile.

But Gigi looked worried. "You never even gained an ounce, Annie. And you'd better check out the hospeetal. The baby does not look like either of you!"

"Is she always like this?" West asked, directing his question straight to Annie as though Gigi wasn't there.

Annie barely smiled. "She's usually funnier."

That wasn't exactly what he meant, but West let it go. None of this was really happening. That had to be it. He had been alone so much he was finally flipping over into a Twilight Zone where one woman after another was going to show up at his door until he finally ran from the house screaming like a lunatic.

Considering that, he gave Annie another long look as she explained to her aunt that Teddy wasn't their baby. Maybe his own private lunacy might not be too bad, if all the women who showed up looked like Annie.

"Well, *ma petite*," Gigi said, "whose baby ees it? I'm afraid I don't understand any of this."

"That makes two of us," West piped in dryly.

Annie ignored him. "The baby is the son of one of my clients. My client abandoned Teddy on West's doorstep and sent me a note asking me to check on him." Annie quickly explained the rest of what had happened that evening, including the part about the bet.

"And you think you will be the better mother?"

"Parent," West corrected quickly. All three of them, including Teddy, turned their heads to look at him. "Better *parent!*"

"Of course," Gigi said swiftly. "You are a handsome man, West Gallagher." West looked embarrassed, and Annie shared a smile with Gigi. "My niece cannot stay here alone. It ees good this house has ample room for her old aunt."

Annie knew she'd feel better with Gigi there, and wondered if that was because she didn't trust West, or because she didn't trust herself. "West? It is all right, isn't it?"

"Oh, she can stay," West said. "Why not?" This was all so crazy, he was past caring about yet another houseguest.

"Maneefique," Gigi said, making West grimace as she slaughtered the word. With a whirl of her silk skirt, Gigi hurried back through the door, calling over her shoulder, "I will get my things."

Not quite believing all this was happening to him, West turned toward Annie. Her hazel eyes were shining with fondness as she watched her aunt leave, but her head was shaking back and forth. "Sometimes I can't quite believe I'm related to her."

That made two of them, West thought. "She brought luggage?" he asked.

"I called her earlier." Her hazel eyes examined him carefully. "It's very nice of you to let her stay."

"I figure I'll be safer with a chaperon in the house."

The edges of Annie's mouth curved upward. "Worried about your virtue?"

"Yep." He smiled that beguiling smile again, the one that had to be responsible for his success on the seminar circuit. She read definite interest in his eyes, and felt a tug inside her that told her she was interested in him, too.

But they were night and day in personality and doomed as a potential couple. He didn't seem to want anyone around him who might become close, and she longed for that in her life. She totally disagreed with the way he encouraged people to seek their hearts' desires without considering the consequences. And she couldn't stand losing another husband, so she wasn't about to set herself up for that kind of heartache. Not that any of that mattered anyway. She had no time for her clients who needed her, where on earth would she find time for a relationship?

For the next three days she was just going to have to ignore the fact that West Gallagher was one appealing hunk. It should be easy enough with Aunt Gigi here to divert her attention, and then she would have Teddy and be gone.

"Your aunt's name," West said quietly, "is it really Gigi?"

"Ginger," Annie told him, keeping her voice just as low. "But she hates it. Says it makes her sound like somebody's pet poodle."

"Is that accent real?"

"Of course not. But it's part of Gigi. I think she's a frustrated actress."

"I heard that," Gigi said loudly, only to be shushed by both West and Annie as she hustled back inside. She dropped a small overnight bag on the floor in front of them and smiled at the drowsy baby, whose heavily lashed eyes were closing. "I have given up acting," she said in a softer voice. "To be a singer ees now—how do you say?—my fantasy, my calling, my…"

"Dream?" West suggested, grinning at Annie.

"Oh, Lord, help," Annie whispered, looking heavenward. "Two of them in the same house."

Gigi beamed, all red lipstick. "So *Monsoor* West, where do I sleep?"

West glanced down at the small piece of luggage, and then looked at Annie. "There's a spare bedroom at the head of the stairs. You can share, or one of you can sleep on the couch down here."

"Lovely." Gigi nodded, picked up the bag, and headed toward the staircase on the far side of the foyer. "Oh, Annie," she said in a loud whisper, turning and walking back to them. "I almost forgot. I have two nightgowns, in case you didn't go home to get something in which to sleep."

"No, that's all right," Annie said, seeing interest spring to life in West's eyes at the mention of nightgowns. "I brought something." She'd had no intention of going around in a nightgown or pajamas in West's house. That would make the situation a little too *intimate.*

"I know what you wear—a T-shirt and shorts to bed. *Non!*" the older woman said, frantic but quiet, plopping her case down on the thick rug and flipping it open. Light glinted off the mirror on the lid. "*Non, non, non.* You will not get a good night's sleep wearing a brassiere— Just zee thing!" Gigi triumphantly held up a black negligee. "You can sleep in this."

Annie could see light through the cloth. Cheeks flushing red, she avoided looking at West. "No," she said tightly. "Not in a stranger's house, Aunt Gigi."

"Oh, please, don't let me stop you," West said. "I've never met a stranger." *Especially not one in a black satin negligee.* He eyed the black shimmer of the delicate material and wondered if Annie wore that kind of thing to sleep when she was at home alone. He could picture her slim, almost willowy body in the gown, her curves gliding against the silk, his hands—

"West, whatever you're thinking, stop." Annie shot him a look that said he was never going to see her in the gown. "You can give that dream up right now."

West threw up his hands in defeat but continued to stare at the negligee.

"But my darling Annie—" Gigi started.

"No!" Annie said, whispering more fiercely because the other woman was still waving the gown as if her niece might change her mind. Worse, West was now staring at her speculatively. "Forget you saw that," she told him sternly.

West and her aunt gave heartfelt sighs of disappointment at the same time. But thankfully, her aunt put her gown back in her case and shut the top. When the older woman had disappeared upstairs, West turned to Annie and grinned.

"She's such a nice woman," he said. "Surely you could have tried to accommodate her a little."

"Dream on, Gallagher," Annie answered sweetly, pulling Teddy's bottle from his grasp. The baby slept peacefully.

"You got him to go to sleep." His voice held admiration.

"Experience," she whispered. "*Know-how.* Since I've got it, Teddy, of course, will be sleeping in my bed."

"Nohow," he said, shaking his head. "No way."

"Oh, Gallagher," she said in mock admiration, "aren't you good verbally?"

"Horizontally, too." He grinned, and she groaned. Teddy stirred, reminding her to keep quieter. "Teddy might need something in the middle of the night. I don't think you'll wake up."

"And how could you possibly know?"

"You'll be too busy dreaming—it is what you do best, right?" Her hazel eyes gleamed triumphantly.

This time it was his turn to groan, and she smiled. But her arms and upper back protested a little under Teddy's weight, so she resumed the argument. "The trouble with you, West, is that you've never learned to compromise."

"And you have?"

"Yep," she agreed amiably. "I'm compromising for Teddy's sake by agreeing to this bet, but you're insisting on having everything your way."

"You're wrong," he said with great assurance. "If I had everything my way, I'd be alone right now."

"Oh, and here I thought we were starting to get along so well," she said, her words hiding her hurt at his abruptness.

His dark eyes narrowed. "The bed in the spare room will fit you and your aunt. Teddy stays with me."

Annie fervently wished she'd slept at the office to-night instead of going home. But then she looked down at Teddy and knew it was destiny for her to be here, helping him. "You'll crush him."

"It's a king-size mattress. Real soft, and lots of room to roll around on." The sexy, sizzling grin that accompanied Gallagher's answer robbed Annie of her breath and her heart skittered.

"Good," she murmured. "Then Teddy and I will be quite comfortable on your bed."

"We're all sharing?" West asked, sounding happier than he ought to sound.

"You're sleeping on the couch."

"My bedroom doesn't have a couch."

"Right." Teddy still in her arms, she walked toward the stairway.

"This isn't settled," West said, following Annie up the stairs.

"Possession is nine-tenths of the law, West, and I'm holding the baby. Cope." Fully aware West was right behind her, Annie opened doors until she found the other bedroom. Heading directly for the bed, which was big enough to live up to West's promise, she gently set Teddy down as close to the middle as she could get, then started situating the pillows so he wouldn't roll off.

West watched her from the doorway, his arms crossed over his chest. Why was he letting her sweep away all the control he'd won over his life? It took him a minute to remember. Oh yes. He was letting her boss him around because he didn't want her getting mad, leaving, and bringing back bad publicity. He didn't want her getting a grip on Teddy and putting him into a foster home.

Spotting the worried expression on West's face, Annie kept herself from smiling. Gallagher was more frightened of her than she was of him. He was going to let her camp out in his bed; she was positive of it.

Once Teddy was safe and settled, Annie faced him. "It's getting late, West."

She meant, West thought, *Get out.* "Does your aunt Gigi know you're sleeping in my room?"

"I'm sure she won't blink her super-deluxe eyelashes when she finds out—as long as you're sleeping somewhere else.''

More tired than he could remember ever being, West gave up. ''All right,'' he said quietly. ''I'll sleep on the couch downstairs. You try to sneak away, I'll hear you.''

Her look of relief made him frown. Apparently she didn't want to be around him any more than he wanted to be around her. That was good, he reminded himself, and the way he wanted it. Annie Robicheaux was one damned pesky female, and the sooner he got her to leave here, the better off he would be.

''Thank you, West,'' she said softly, truly grateful he'd finally given in without too much of a fight. ''You won't be sorry. Teddy will probably wake up during the night, and this way, you'll get all the rest you need.'' She gave him a long look. ''I promise I won't take him away. And if there's one thing I never break, West, it's my word.''

Somehow, even though West didn't trust anyone in the system, he knew Annie would be there in the morning. As he looked in his dresser for what he would need the next day, he had to wonder if he was starting to like her.

Just a little.

West jolted awake as his hand slid off his chest and hit the edge of the coffee table. Disoriented, he sat up and stared around him in the dusky light. He must have fallen asleep on the couch again. He did that a lot lately, usually because he'd had no reason to go ahead upstairs to his lonely king-size bed.

Yawning, he got up and went for the stairs, half stumbling up them. His eyes were almost shut and he kept them that way, hoping to maintain the hazy state he was in so he'd go back to sleep the second he hit the mattress.

Entering his room, barely registering the dim light of early morning seeping in through the blinds, something in the back of his mind told him that it was now Saturday, and he wasn't booked anywhere till five that afternoon, so he could sleep as late as he wanted and it still wouldn't matter.... He threw himself down on top of the sheets a foot or so from the top of his extra-long bed.

"What are you doing in here?" came a terrified, feminine screech inches from him, along with a baby's cry. In total shock, West reeled his arms backward and fell off the bed onto the floor with a thump. At about the same time, everything came back to him with startling clarity. Someone was sleeping in his bed....

And it wasn't Goldilocks.

"How can you be trusted if you can't be trusted to be trusted?" Annie asked, half asleep and fully in shock.

"What are you talking about?" he asked, a little too forcefully, still on the floor. He ran his fingers through his hair and blinked, trying to get his bearings.

"With the baby, I mean. How can you be trusted with Teddy, if you can't be trusted to not come in here?" Her voice seemed very loud, even compared to Teddy's crying. "How can you tell people how wonderful you are and then do something like this?"

"I'm not that wonderful, and I forgot about you!" he yelled in protest—not that Annie seemed to be listening. As she continued to rant, he got up off the floor, slowly coming out of his ozoned state. She flipped on the light, giving him a full view of her.

Her T-shirt stretched over her breasts, outlining her curves, making the totally modest garment seem more enticing than it had any right to be. Her legs were covered to mid-thigh by a pair of champagne satin tap pants that didn't go with the T-shirt at all. He could just imagine the top half of that lingerie set—and her in it.

Aunt Gigi chose that minute to burst into the room, and maybe, West thought, that was a good thing.

"Oh, my poor babee!"

"I'm all right," he said, but Gigi was already heading toward Teddy, whom both women began to comfort. Telling himself he was stupid for feeling neglected, West started toward his dresser to get a pair of jeans, before he remembered that they were all in the wash and that had been the first thing he'd planned to do when he got up.

"Gallagher," Annie said warningly, "you stay on your side of the room—" Suddenly she giggled. "Oh, my." She laughed some more as she continued to stare at him, and then Gigi stared, and she giggled, too. Teddy, sensing the dissipating anger in the room, began to quiet.

Glaring at them all, West, frozen where he was at the foot of the bed, remembered. He remembered that his pants were downstairs where he'd taken them off last night before they'd all gone to sleep, and he remembered that all he was wearing now was a pair of cotton boxer shorts that were a size too small. And as if that weren't embarrassing enough, they were covered with—

He groaned. *Now* he remembered. Cherubs. Pale, rosy-faced little cherubs floating around on a sky-blue background. Babies. He glanced down and for one long second, they all looked like Teddy.

He was going insane.

Annie stared at him with a wide grin on her face. "Oh, please, let me guess. A girlfriend's Valentine's Day gift?"

"My brother's wife sent them to me," he said, grabbing the sheet off the bed and wrapping it around him. "She thought women would find me irresistible in them and fall in love with me, if you must pry into my private—"

"Oh, *non, non,* we are not going to pry into your privates!" Gigi pushed at Annie, who walked with her toward the door. Annie started laughing so hard Teddy was almost bouncing off her chest. She turned her head to look back at West.

"I was wrong, wasn't I?" she asked. "You *can* catch cuteness. In those shorts, you're adorable."

West scowled. "My sister-in-law thinks I ought to get married," he said irritably. "She thinks I'll be a lot happier. *I* personally think she must be crazy."

Despite her aunt's urging, Annie stopped long enough to turn, her eyes sparkling over the top of Teddy's head. "Gallagher, take my word for it—your sister-in-law has it wrong. It's not the shorts when it comes to winning a woman, it's what's inside that counts.''

"Ooh la la!" Gigi interrupted, smiling.

"Inside the man, Aunt Gigi." Annie gave her a mock frown. "You have a dirty mind."

Laughing, Gigi pulled at Annie again, and they disappeared into the hallway with Teddy, closing the door behind them. Ignoring the gales of laughter floating through the door, West stared after Annie for a minute.

He'd been kicked out of his bed over a baby. He'd been dictated to in his own home. He'd been caught in a pair of shorts that would make him the laughing-stock of New Orleans if word got out. No more.

Hurrying to his door, he locked it. After he showered and put on a pair of dress slacks, he was going downstairs and damn well get control back over his life.

He held on to that determination—right until he got to the bottom of the stairs twenty minutes later and found Gigi with her bags walking out the door, with an anxious Annie trying to convince her not to leave while she held and gave Teddy his bottle.

"She can't go," West muttered. If she went, how was he going to resist Annie? "This cannot be happening."

"But it is," Annie snapped in a soft voice, remembering the baby in her arms. "Gigi doesn't seem to believe we need her here."

"Even after that commotion this morning, you can't tell?" West asked Gigi.

"Tell that you are no more interested in Annie than she ees in you?" Gigi waved her arms. "Tell that Annie ees as safe here with you as she would be in my very own home?" She shook her head in disgust. "Children, please. I have better things to do than ba-bee-sit two grown people who know exactly what they want—and eet isn't each other."

"Well, as long as we have that straight," Annie said firmly, looking at West.

West looked back, and then he turned to Gigi. Fully dressed, the older woman was staring at him with heavily made-up eyes she hadn't had twenty minutes ago. How had she done all that to herself so fast? He rubbed his chin wearily, feeling the stubble of a second day of beard. He hadn't even had the time to shave. "I think I'm getting a little tired of you two telling me what I want—"

Gigi blinked her long, black, fake eyelashes at him. "Are you saying you do want my *Annee?*"

"No!" he said quickly. Gigi shot him a knowing look, and he scowled. "I'm not saying anything— that's the problem. If I'd said more since this began, maybe I wouldn't have lost all control in my own home."

"So what ees it you want to control anyway?" Gigi asked him. "If it ees *Annee,* then you must want her around."

In total frustration, West turned to Annie. "Aren't you going to say anything?"

Annie shook her head so that her honey-gold hair

fell around her shoulders in waves. "You're getting in enough trouble all by yourself. Besides, aren't you the one who's in to mind control seminars?" She waved her hand at Gigi. "Have at it. Make me a believer. Get her to stay."

"Gigi, we need you here," he said, meaning it. Standing next to Annie, smelling roses wafting from her, seeing her in a fresh T-shirt and jeans that skimmed her lean curves and had him remembering that she'd slept in his bed last night, alone—well, all that made him want her aunt in his house to keep him on the straight and narrow.

Because if he didn't stay on the straight and narrow and if he started letting himself remember that he almost enjoyed having Annie around, he might start envisioning all sorts of stupid things like maybe trying to make this arrangement permanent—which, of course, it could never be. Any fool could tell Annie was meant to have children, and he wasn't cut out for permanent fatherhood.

Gigi reached up and patted his cheek. "You don't have the problem with Annie you think you do, *Monsoor* West Gallagher, if you would only settle down and realize it." She wiggled her fingers in the air. "Anyway, to be a singer, that ees my dream, and I need to be out pursuing it. Isn't that what you tell everyone, West?"

Frowning, Annie hoisted Teddy up in her arms. "Aunt Gigi, you weren't saying any of this last night."

"Ah! But last night, I had not read West's book. It ees an eye-opener."

"Where did you get his book?" Annie asked, eyeing West suspiciously.

"Don't look at me," West said. "I make people *buy* copies at the stores."

"From his study." Gigi grinned. "I will check in, children, and give you a progress report on how I make out becoming a singer. Do not fight too much." Blowing them a kiss, she picked up her bag, paused without turning, and kicked the door shut behind her.

"Gallagher," Annie said immediately, turning to him. "This is all your fault!"

"Now how do you figure that?"

"Aunt Gigi has never in her whole life bailed out on me when I needed her. She reads your book and just like that—" Annie snapped her fingers "—she's gone. For the life of me I can't understand what it is in those pages that makes people go off chasing pots of gold! First Marcia and now my aunt. I just can't see it!"

From what he'd seen of Gigi thus far, West had the feeling this wasn't the first time the woman had chased rainbows, but he was gentleman enough not to point that out to Annie. "Is this going to be an argument?" he asked. "Because if it is, I haven't had my coffee yet." Passing her, he headed toward the kitchen, confident she would follow.

He was right. He heard her gentle sigh behind him as he regarded the coffeepot, plugged in and brewing, with relief and reached for a mug. "All I ever tell people," he explained, "is that they can have their dreams if they want them badly enough."

"Then you are telling them a lie, Gallagher," she said softly.

There was a dispirited tone in her voice that made West turn to her. As Teddy played with her hair, she looked back at West with her beautiful hazel eyes so full of hurt that West almost couldn't stand it. "Why do you think it's a lie, Annie?" he asked quietly.

"You can want something with all your heart, but some dreams are not meant to happen."

"You're wrong," West told her. The coffee whooshed through the filter and the baby gurgled as West and Annie held a standoff with their eyes. "I made my dreams come true, and I started with nothing. No money, no family—" He paused solemnly. "And no hope."

Annie broke their deadlocked gaze to stare down at Teddy, and West thought she might be close to tears. But then she blinked and furiously shook her head, sending hair into Teddy's grasp, much to the baby's delight. "Nothing in the world will make me believe in the panacea you're pushing, West, or that people are better off seeking it."

"Nothing?" he asked. Taking a few seconds to pour himself a cup of coffee and think, he turned back to her. "Why, Annie..." he said, mug in hand, his lips twisting as he bit back a smile. "Are you handing me another challenge?"

Annie's heart leapt and turned over. She wasn't. She was. She wanted to run out of West's house before he invaded her private world and tore apart her carefully schooled emotions, but if she did, she wouldn't get Teddy, wouldn't help Marcia, and she'd also lose her chance to prove to West how wrong he was for making people believe in magic. She gave him a slow nod. "I am definitely throwing down the glove."

"Then I accept," he said, his fingers reaching out and stroking Teddy's head, brushing at the same time against strands of her hair and her collarbone. Annie's insides began a slow meltdown.

"By the time I'm done helping you," West said, "I promise you your dream is going to come true— as long as you promise me you want it more than anything."

"Oh, I do," she said. *If he only knew.* "Not that it will help."

With all his heart, West believed in hopes and dreams and in the strength of character of people to achieve what they wanted. He wanted to make Annie believe what he did, because her eyes and her voice told him she had pain deep inside her, and he hoped if he helped her get her dream, her ensuing happiness would force that pain out of her heart. If the world had one more happy person in it, so much the better. That was his philosophy, and that was why he held his seminars.

His helping Annie had nothing to do with the fact that he wanted her in his bed, he swore.

"So, Annie," he said with a smile that had been proven to please, "tell me your dream."

Cuddling Teddy, Annie, still filled with doubts, took a minute to reconsider. Sharing her dream with West meant baring her soul, and she didn't want to get that close to him. Why bother, when it was so

obvious how different they were and that they had no
future together? Besides, if there was a way for her
to have what she wanted, she would have found it by
now. West couldn't achieve the impossible.

"I don't think this is a good idea," she told him.

"C'mon," he cajoled. "You can't throw anything
at me that I haven't already heard in my seminars or
been through in life. So tell me your dream, Annie.
There isn't anything I can't personally help you get."

Annie sputtered and began to laugh, which made
Teddy grin, too, but bewildered West. She shook her
head. "Oh, West, I'm sorry, but I can't let this one
slip by. You really should have shut up while you
were ahead and I was trying to be fair to you."

Just like the night before, another sense of impend-
ing doom fell over West. "Was it something I said?"

"About helping me get my dream yourself?" She
waited until he nodded. "Okay, West. My dream—
the one thing I want most in the world—is to have
my very own baby."

His mouth dropped open.

She grinned. "Handle that one all by yourself. I
dare you."

5

After all the seminars West had given and the impromptu questions he'd answered, he could only think of one thing to do now as he looked into Annie's challenging, laughing eyes—bail out. Annie was right. That was one dream he wasn't going anywhere near personally, and she'd definitely gotten the better of him in this battle of the wits. He ought to admit defeat and take his failure like a man. But, of course, his male pride wouldn't let him do that.

"Well, this is a first," he drawled slowly.

Annie's bright grin hid years of loneliness and wanting. "I hate to say I told you so, West, but really."

"It's a first," he repeated, "but that doesn't mean your dream is impossible. I can still personally help you make your dream come true."

To Annie's eyes, West's expression had turned almost devilish, and her heart skittered. To personally help her achieve her dream meant only one thing.

"It was a joke, West. A play on words." She backed up.

"You don't want me to personally help you get a baby?"

"Yes…" But they were all alone here—what was she saying? "I mean no!" She *was* in trouble. "The last I looked, West, my dream didn't have you in it."

He grinned more widely.

"Honestly. No offense to you. There aren't *any* men in my dream, just a baby."

"You're going to require at least *one* man in your dream if you're going to get that baby—or didn't you know that?"

"Very funny." Why had she even started this?

His eyes crinkled at the sides with amusement. "So are you going to let me help?"

"Why would you get involved?" she asked, her tone serious. "You said you don't want children."

"And I meant it." Hearing in her voice how important this was to Annie, West didn't have the heart to keep teasing her. "But I did say I would help you go after your dream. You still want me to, don't you?"

Did she? If she believed in what he was doing, she might have said yes immediately, but as it was… "I think my dream is better off buried," she told him quietly. "I examined every angle I could come up with, but affording a baby and continuing to do the work I'm doing is impossible."

West missed nothing. "By work, you mean helping people like Marcia, don't you? What do they call that—pro bono?"

She nodded slowly. Teddy erupted in a string of syllables that sounded like a protest.

''Are we that boring, sweet thing?'' she asked Teddy, putting him down in his nearby basket and handing him a rattle. He lay on his back, kicked, and let loose with another stream of syllables. But for the first time since yesterday Annie's mind wasn't on Teddy—it was on the baby she might have.

Might have had, she corrected. West seemed so certain he could help her, but really, once he understood her situation, even he would see there was no chance of her ever achieving her dream.

''Really, West, if there was some way I could afford a child of my own and still help people—really help, like I'm going to return to doing once Teddy is situated, I would have found it by now,'' she told him. ''But things being as they are, surely even you can see that I can't do both. So tell me, how are you going to personally help me make my dream come true?''

''Have some coffee,'' he urged. ''Sit down, and we'll talk.''

The two of them got coffee and sat down at the kitchen table, Annie next to Teddy's basket where she could watch the baby play. For a few seconds she did, wistfully, but then she looked at West.

Dare she hope for a miracle from the dream chaser that was within West? Could he help her make her dream come true without her losing herself in the bargain?

''Why a baby, Annie?'' West asked. His dark eyes captivated her. Sometimes they were the gentle, hurt eyes of a lost, lonely boy, and sometimes, like now, they were the world-seasoned eyes of a weary old man.

"I was married once, several years ago—but not for long," she said, and then lowered her gaze from his, not really comfortable exposing her soul to him. West reached over and touched her hand encouragingly. All he did was cover her fingers with his own, but there was something about his skin, the way the heat permeated the coolness of her hand, that made Annie feel comforted, as though he understood her hesitancy.

She slipped her hand away from his in a move of self-preservation. No sense in letting the dream chaser get under her skin. "Jean-Pierre had a three-year-old daughter by another marriage. After a year, he left me for someone else and took his daughter with him. I thought of Mariette as my own." She lowered her eyes again. "Silly of me, of course."

West's gut clenched. Someone had walked away from Annie, and she wanted a baby to fill the emptiness left behind.

"Are you still in love with him?" he asked, needing to know at the same time he swore to himself he would not get emotionally involved with a woman whose fondest dream was to have a child.

"No!" she said, her eyelashes sweeping open in surprise. Just as swiftly, her face grew suspicious. "Do you ask everyone in your seminars questions like that?"

"Sure." And he would—he just wouldn't have cared so much about the answer.

That worried him. Was he just going through the

motions of caring during his seminars? Or had he not known what caring was until now, here, with Annie?

"Have you been alone ever since your divorce?" he asked, preferring not to think about why he was asking.

"Not really." She smiled wryly. "I've had Aunt Gigi." She smiled at his look. "Lucky me, huh?"

West thought about how he'd spent all his years in foster care, yearning for someone who was really related to him to come into his life. "Yeah," he nodded, sipping coffee. "You were lucky. Your parents passed on early?"

"Passed on me, more like it."

That hurt-little-boy look West had came and went so suddenly Annie thought she'd imagined it. But then when West got up from the table and walked toward the sink with his coffee cup, she remembered the story of his beginnings in his book. He'd been abandoned, too—under different circumstances, perhaps, but no less left behind. When she'd read that, she'd passed it off as publicity hype, but now she knew she'd been mistaken—the pain she'd just seen on his face had been too real.

"What do you mean, passed on you?" he asked, his back to her as he topped off his coffee.

"I was a 'love child' of the late sixties—my parents never married. From what Aunt Gigi tells me, I'd just turned three and was starting to get a little hard to handle—"

He turned, grinning, once again the charismatic man as he leaned against the counter. "Nothing's changed in twenty-some years, I see."

"You're no good at humor, West. Do you want to hear my life's story or not?"

West nodded slowly, once more serious, so she shifted her position to talk to him comfortably. He had that intense, wise-old-man look back on his face. West could shift his moods faster than a crooked defendant.

"Where was I?" she wondered out loud. "So when Mother decided she 'wasn't into parenting' anymore, she hitchhiked off alone to the good life in California. My father was chanting one of his mantras when a higher power made him see the light and took himself home to South Carolina—alone."

"He joined the ministry?"

She shook her head. "His higher power was money. His own parents promised him all the money he could ever want if he would just reform and enter the family business."

Swearing under his breath, West threw the rest of his coffee into the sink. No amount of heated brew could warm the cold he felt inside at another child left behind, and this time for money. "Where did your aunt fit into this?"

"She's Mother's older sister. Believe it or not, when my parents split up, they agreed that Aunt Gigi was the only one they knew who could take me."

"She did a great job," West said. "You were lucky."

Annie's heart mourned for him, and she wished she'd never made any cracks earlier about her Aunt Gigi. He was right. She'd been so very lucky compared to him.

"So," he said suddenly, "getting back to your dream—why not just get pregnant?"

"I have to be able to support the child, while I help the poor." She brushed away something on the table, her eyes averted. She'd never forgive herself for worrying more about building her bank account than being there for Marcia. "But if I continue to work with very little income, I wind up unable to afford having a child."

West didn't know what to think. Annie had a heart, and unfortunately, so far, it was at the expense of her dream.

"Where does your altruistic streak come from?"

This time Annie did meet his eyes, to see if he was criticizing or making fun of her. There was only interest in them. Well, good, because he was about to get an earful.

"My husband cheated, left me, and then sued for alimony. Alimony! And since I'd been stupid enough to let him stay at home and pursue his *dream*—" she enunciated the word carefully to make sure West understood how she felt "—of becoming a famous painter, while I worked two jobs to support our family, he ended up getting alimony for six months so he had time to 'get back on his feet.'" The memory still burned, and she took a deep breath to calm down. "I ended up paying him because I didn't have good legal help. After that, I swore no one was ever going to have to wind up paying for being a good, responsible person because they couldn't afford the best help they could find."

She was upset. West knew if he went to Annie, he

would take her in his arms and tell her how great he thought she was. Add that to the attraction he felt to her, and the baby she wanted, and it was a dangerous combination. He stayed at the sink.

"Not all men are like Jean-Pierre," he said carefully.

"I know that."

"Then you could have your dream by finding yourself another husband."

Her eyebrow quirked upward in a "yeah, right" look. "Do you know what I'd be doing right now if we weren't in the middle of this crazy bet?"

He shook his head.

"Legal briefs. Interviews. Just plain paperwork. I have a mountain of files on my desk that need to be put away. Just how would I find the time to nurture another relationship?"

"The same way you would find the time to nurture a baby."

That stopped her, but only for a few seconds. "That's my point, isn't it, West? There is no way to make my dream come true."

"A father would help. Children need two parents, Annie."

Her gaze met his. "No. Children only need love. It can come from anywhere."

He shook his head. "You may see it that way because of your aunt Gigi, but I don't. A child needs a mother, a father, and a forever."

"We both lost both our parents," she said, "and in the long run, it didn't matter for us, did it?"

"It mattered to me," he said slowly, meaningfully.

"Your past always influences how you are now. My past is why I don't want to try for my own family."

Annie hurt inside for West, and for what he was going to miss. "And *my* past is partly why I want my own so very much. But what happens to you if you fall in love with someone, West? Does your opinion about having a child change then?"

He shook his head. "Love can die just as fast as it's born. Couples divorce, and all that's left behind are the victims. I won't be responsible for bringing a child into this world only to go through what I did— the foster home, the lack of parents." The feeling of not being tied to anyone, anywhere. The feeling that no one would ever really care about him enough never to leave him.

"Did you ever see your parents again after they left you?" she asked, trying to understand the full extent of his pain. "Did you find out why they left you?"

West had sketched out how he'd been abandoned in his book, but now, his arms crossed over his chest and his eyes focusing on something far away—memories?—he filled Annie in on what he'd learned from his reunion the previous year with his father, mother and brother. His father had been an alcoholic, and upon West's mother's ultimatum, had chosen the road and the bottle over his wife and sons. His mother had tried, but been unable to earn enough to support him and his brother and left them at the county home so they could eat, believing the "system" that had promised her she could get them back as soon as she got her life in order.

But his mother couldn't find a good enough job, and the judge had placed him and Matthew in foster care, officially taking them away from her. As if losing his parents wasn't bad enough, he'd been torn away from his beloved brother, and only recently, after twenty years, been reunited. But the years had taken their toll on both him and Matthew, and his family was now nothing more than friendly strangers.

"If having a child is your dream, Annie, by all means, have one," West finished. "But choose the man wisely. Give this child of yours a fighting chance at having some real happiness and sense of belonging and security. Do that for the kids we were." He paused. "Please?"

While she listened she had been watching Teddy, but now their gazes merged. Her eyes were wide and wet with tears. Concerned, West walked to her, hunkered down, and drew his fingers across her cheek to wipe away the tears, flashing her a smile. "Hey, for a dream chaser, I didn't turn out that badly, did I? I ended up with a heart."

A badly bruised one, Annie thought, trying to ignore the rush of sensual feeling evoked from West's touch that mingled with the compassion she was feeling for him. West had been left entirely alone, and now, in his own way, he was trying to help people—even if it was in the rather peculiar fashion of chasing their fantasies—so he could alleviate some of the loneliness from his childhood. He was a good man at heart.

Not to mention sexy and absolutely appealing.

She blinked back tears and brushed her cheeks with

the flat of her hand. "That was silly of me, West, but it's so sad. You're all alone."

"Now I was just thinking the exact opposite," he said, looking pointedly at Teddy and then at her as he stood.

"You know what I mean. You aren't in real contact with your parents, you don't know your brother anymore, and you don't want a wife and kids. I'm afraid you're never going to find happiness if you don't have love in your life."

"I'm happy," he protested. "So don't worry about me." He went back to the counter and rinsed out his coffee cup, wanting to put some distance between them. He *was* happy, he repeated to himself. "Besides, we aren't talking about my desires here, are we?"

"No," she said softly, taking a deep breath.

Good thing, too, West thought, because she wouldn't want to hear what he'd been desiring since his fingers had made contact with Annie's soft skin. Her. Touching her. Tasting her peach-colored lips.

Damn. He wished he hadn't discovered Annie had a caring side to her that could extend past babies all the way to him. He really wished he hadn't found that out.

Work. He needed to concentrate on what he did best—guiding Annie into fulfilling her dream.

"Since I believe what I believe about babies needing two parents," he said, "and since I really want to help you get your dream, that means only one thing."

"What?" Annie asked, clueless.

"We're going to have to find you a forever kind of guy." He grinned at her. "One that dotes on and worships you and the kiddie-to-be, and wants a permanent place in your home." And in her heart, West added silently. A part of him protested vehemently the idea of marrying her off, but since he wasn't volunteering for this job—no way, not him—what choice did he have?

"No, West." Annie rose from her seat and picked up Teddy, who was getting restless in the basket. "Remember what I told you? I don't have time for a relationship. And besides, this is my dream, and I'm having it exactly the way I want it. One baby, one mama. Just like you said, too many marriages end in divorce—and you were right. If I do have a baby, I'm not having some creep in my life forever, wrecking my dream come true."

"Then I can't help you."

Rocking the baby from side to side, Annie smiled over Teddy's head. "Ha! I knew it. I knew you would find some way out of this. You are a charlatan, taking people's money for nothing."

"That hurt," West said.

"Admit it."

"I really do help people, Annie."

She took a long look at Teddy, and then met West's eyes, all the desire, the want, and the hope of the last few years centered in hers. "Then prove it, West. Put aside your personal beliefs and help me get my baby."

Everything in West warred on the side of insisting she do it the right way, or he didn't want any part in this. But he had a feeling, whether she thought she could afford a baby or not, that eventually Annie was going to have one. If it happened while he was around, maybe he could convince her that her baby would need both its parents in its life. Happily married if possible, but even he didn't believe in that big of a dream.

But then again, what if he didn't convince her of a thing, and he helped her achieve her dream anyway? Then he would have done the one thing he swore he would never do, even if indirectly, and that was to bring a child into this world who might end up suffering for the lack of a parent.

"I can't go against what I believe in, Annie."

"It's so easy to stand up in front of a roomful of people and rally them, isn't it, West? 'C'mon everyone, pay your money, and I'll give you the universal cure. Believe in yourself, and do it yourself.' But when it comes to truly sitting down and making the effort to help someone, one-on-one, you'd rather not get involved. Am I right?"

West shifted uncomfortably. Was Annie right? Was that all he was doing when he gave his seminars—cheerleading? He thought in this age of people who were losing hope that motivating *was* helping them. But if he believed Annie, it wasn't enough. "Let me think about this for a while."

Annie took a deep breath. He'd think, and then say no. She told herself she shouldn't be disappointed—but deep down inside, she was. For a few minutes she'd let herself believe in West and his faith in dreams. Dumb.

"Well, while you're doing all your deep thinking, West, Teddy should have some fresh air and sunshine. I'm going to take him for a walk.'' She smiled. "And that's a point for me. I'll jot it down on the way out.''

"I'll go with you.'' After their talk, West no longer believed she would steal Teddy away, but his years with the system made it difficult for him to totally trust. "But first, I was hoping to look in my registration records for Marcia's address, and then make some calls to see if I can get someone to hunt her down.'' He paused and added, almost gleefully, "Point for me.''

Mercy, Annie thought, at this rate every single point was going to count. She might as well use what she had. "I found out last night at the grocery where Marcia works that she quit on Thursday, and the manager at her apartment told me she said she was going on vacation.''

"Then she is coming back.'' West's eyebrows went into slashes. "When were you planning on telling me this?''

"Right now.'' She smiled and held up two fingers. "Two points for all my legwork.''

It went on like that between them, back and forth, for the rest of the morning and early afternoon. Seemingly, the minute Annie thought of something that would be good for Teddy, West would come up with something equally important, or vice versa, both of them racking up points.

West tried to withdraw from both Annie and Teddy during the time the three of them spent together, but it was difficult. Just as he had himself convinced that he would be happy if the private detective he'd contacted found Marcia within the hour, he glimpsed Annie encouraging Teddy to crawl and found himself mesmerized. Just as he tried to go over his notes for his five o'clock seminar, Teddy held out his arms to West, and started crying with huge, wet eyes that touched his heart. Just as he'd convinced himself that he wasn't going to help Annie after all, the thought of the baby she might have going through life without a father because he didn't butt into her life and change it haunted him.

And finally he made his decision, reminding himself he was in no way getting personally involved with either her or Teddy. Dealing with both of them was merely a job he had to fit in between his seminars and working on plans for his infomercial. A temporary job, not meant to last forever. He didn't believe in forevers.

"All right, Annie," he said, walking back into the living room where she was with Teddy. "I'll bite the bait. I have to go to a seminar now, but starting tomorrow, you and I are going to work on your dream."

Sitting on the floor, Annie was changing Teddy on a plastic pad she'd bought the night before. Hurriedly snapping up the baby's romper, she picked him up and stared at West, her jaw opening and her hazel eyes stunned—both at his announcement and at his clothes. His expensive-looking suit was chosen to show him off to perfect advantage, cut just right and in deep blues that brought out his eyes and black hair. If he was handsome in his regular clothes, he was powerful in these. Powerful and—okay, she would think it—*charismatic*. And sexy.

"You're going to help me achieve my dream exactly as I've planned it?" He'd avoided the topic since they'd dropped it that morning, and she figured that was the end of that. "I have a baby, I continue to be able to work, and I don't have to have a father involved?"

Oh, great, West thought, she had to add the last. Now he was going to have to almost lie, since he wasn't about to let her get away with consigning the baby's father to oblivion. "I'm going to prove to you I'm not a fake," he said carefully, "and that I really care."

He really cared. Never taking her eyes off him, Annie kissed the top of the baby's head for luck. "West, I don't truly believe you can do any better than I did on my own, but if you really do make this work for me, I would be forever grateful."

"Enough to do a testimonial in my infomercial?"

"Don't push it," she warned, returning his smile.

"So we'll work together on this." Leaving the living room for his study, he stuffed some papers inside the open briefcase on his desk, closed it, and then turned to find her and Teddy standing at the door. "Just remember one thing."

She waited, her eyes raised in question.

"I'm not the man for the job."

"Of course," she said softly. "You've made that perfectly clear." And he had.

For a few seconds she wondered why she was agreeing to let him help her when she didn't believe for one minute he'd do any better than she had with her life. The answer came swiftly. She was letting him help her because deep down, desperately, she wanted West to think he was really helping people, because he needed people in his life so much, and he didn't even know it. Deep down, she was starting to really care about the man.

"So where do we start?" she asked, unable to stop herself from being pulled into his spell.

"I'll have to make up a plan of action based on my theories. We'll get started either when I get back, or tomorrow, first thing." Taking his briefcase off his desk, he walked over to stand in front of her. "We will, that is, if you'll promise me you won't turn Teddy in to the authorities while I'm doing my seminar?"

"You really think I could listen this morning to everything that happened to you as a kid and still do the same thing they did?" She gazed at him, hurt in her hazel eyes. "You must think I don't have a heart at all, West."

"I'm going to trust you," he said softly.

Annie didn't know what to say. West was going to believe in her, and she knew how hard that would be for him, what with who she was, and who he was, and the baby's future they both held in their hands. "I'll be here with Teddy when you come home," she whispered. "I promise."

West's hands rose to rest on her shoulders, and taking care not to crush Teddy, he leaned down and gave her a quick, feather-soft kiss that melted her heart and made her wish that they were different people than who they were. Slipping by her, he left the study without another word, and seconds later, she heard the front door shut.

Lord, her bleeding heart was going to be the end of her. She was about to let herself believe in him, and West wasn't going to be able to help her, and her heart was going to get broken all over again. How had a simple bet over mothering a baby gotten so darned complicated—and dangerous?

6

———◆———

"So, Teddy, I have a problem," West muttered to the baby, who was trying to sit up by himself in the safety of the playpen, which, along with a car seat, West had gotten on a trip to the mall after his seminar was over the previous evening. "How do I help Annie get her wish without letting her get near another man?"

Hanging on to the tightly woven sides of the pen and having himself a gay old time, Teddy drooled and let go, falling sideways with a gurgle against a wealth of plush sofa pillows West had stuck in there.

"Yeah, I know. We're both clueless." West sighed, long and hard, throwing his notebook down beside him on the sofa. "I guess that makes me as brainy as a six-month-old." It was not a pleasant thought.

His trouble in forming a plan had started last evening, when, after he'd returned home and found Annie still there, just as she'd promised, he'd realized that not only was he attracted to her, he could trust her. The fact that she was going along with his wishes made him really want to reciprocate by coming up with some way for her to have her dream that didn't force his ideals on her. And that was the catch.

He'd mulled over different possibilities after she and Teddy had gone upstairs to his bed, but none seemed right and, finally, around one in the morning, he'd given up. This morning had been filled with laundry and food shopping, since his normally not-well-stocked cupboards—he ate out a lot—were getting bare. And then Annie, early that afternoon, had left Teddy with him to go to her office, stating with a smile she hoped he was ready to go to work on a baby when she returned that evening.

Go to work on a baby with Annie. The very thought conjured up images that had him sweating all afternoon.

And now it was already seven. He'd spent most of the time she'd been gone thinking about how to help Annie achieve her dream, had even come up with some possible solutions for her money problems. But each time he got to the point where she actually conceived the child, he got hung up. The more he tried to make her dream come true, the more knotted up inside he became.

He should never have kissed her.

"Damn," he said under his breath, picking up his notebook again. This whole thing was so complicated. He *was* only supposed to be the motivator, helping people believe they could have their dream. Despite what Annie thought, he'd never claimed to be able to overcome anyone's obstacles. Yet he would have to slay Annie's dragons for her if he were to ever make her believe she could have her dream come true, because she'd given up hope.

And he hated it when people had no hope. Life without hope that you could have something you dreamed of was living with poverty of the soul. He knew. He'd been there.

Damn it, there was always a way, he told himself, feeling anger at his inadequacy heating within him. He would just have to find it.

Annie had to smile when she returned from her office at eight o'clock and slipped through the rear door of West's home. Not only had West left the door unlocked for her, he'd left the front, the garage, and the kitchen lights on, as well. So much for worrying about whether he really wanted her to return or not.

Although she could hear West talking to Teddy in the living room, and she was dying to see the baby again, she went directly to West's bedroom instead, mainly to shower, but also to avoid having to talk to West for as long as possible. After discussing his seminar and the baby's new things last night, and Teddy's future and West's childhood that morning, she was awfully afraid that eventually, if he couldn't produce his "plan," they would have nothing left to talk about except the kiss. And *that* she didn't want to discuss with him.

Nor did she even want to think about how good the kiss had felt, or how much she wanted him to kiss her again. There was no future for them, no compromising on the way they wanted their lives.

Ready to face the inevitable, Annie padded barefoot out of the bedroom, and headed downstairs. She was glad she'd gone to the office today. The work had taken her mind off West, and renewed her determination not to leave without Teddy in her arms tomorrow evening, the end of the bet. After she'd discovered two other pro bono cases that had been buried in her avalanche of paperwork and forgotten, her conscience was throbbing painfully.

Pushing her honey-gold hair behind her ears, she reached the bottom of the stairs. West was walking with Teddy against his shoulder toward the playpen when the three of them met in the hallway. Seeing the look in her eyes, he handed the baby to her.

''Where have you been?'' he asked. ''I thought you'd be home a couple hours ago.''

''Careful, West,'' she said softly, walking into the living room and easing down onto the softness of the sofa with a drowsy Teddy in her arms. ''Or I'll think you missed me.''

''What I missed doesn't matter. It's what you missed.'' West sat on the couch, too, reclining with a groan of contentment and leaving her to wonder what had happened while she was gone. His shirt was stained. Had Teddy had a solitary food fight, with West as the target? With his mussed hair and the growl on his face, Annie found she had to smile at him.

And then he angled his thigh so that it brushed against her knee, and all her amusement at the rough afternoon he must have had playing daddy ceased. Every time he shifted, hot tremors ran up her leg and curled around her insides. She swallowed.

"If taking care of Teddy and worrying about me is getting to you, West, I'll be happy to call the bet off and take him home with me." *Soon. Please. End this agony.*

He put an end to that idea with a shake of his head. "We're in this together, until the end of the bet."

"Then what did I miss?" She sounded cranky, even to herself.

"About an hour ago, Marcia called. But I was giving Teddy a bath after his dinner—he got kind of dirty—"

"I see," she said, pointing to West's shirt.

"—and I couldn't leave him. The machine picked it up."

Annie felt like cursing. She should have been here. Since about six she'd been doing nothing but thinking about West and how, no matter what he came up with, there just weren't enough hours in her day or money in her bank account to do the job she wanted to do for people and have a child, too. There just wasn't. And there was no sense in hoping that while she'd been gone West had worked up any kind of plan that would change a thing in her life.

"Oh, West, I'm so sorry. What did she say?"

"She hopes Teddy isn't being a problem and she's definitely going to be back by next Saturday."

"But that's a whole week!"

West's eyebrows arched. "Tell me something I don't already know. Your aunt called, too. She said something about passing her audition."

"What audition?"

"At the Café Lauree in the French Quarter. She's

having rehearsals every day and performing free on Tuesday evening. If she's a hit, she'll be hired on there for two nights a week. So quote, 'Don't expect me to drop by anytime soon.'" He closed his eyes and yawned. "And we're both invited. She's even lined up a sitter for us. It'd be nice if we went."

If she wasn't so darned aware of West as a man, Annie doubted his saying they should go would have affected her at all. But the kiss the day before and his closeness now made her cautious. What was he up to? It was crystal clear that both of them knew where they stood with each other, so why was he trying to get closer to her?

"This sounds suspiciously like a rigged-up date, West, and I don't like the sounds of it at all."

"Rigged-up date?" Opening his eyes, West shifted his entire body away from her as he sat up straight. "In case you haven't noticed, dating isn't one of my priorities and getting you married off isn't one of your aunt's."

That was true.

"It's her dream, Annie. Don't you want to be there to share it with her?"

"I was there," she replied, "when no one would buy her paintings." She wasn't upset at his question because he really didn't know Gigi's background. "I was also there each time when she came home disappointed because she got only bit parts in the local plays. I think maybe Aunt Gigi would understand if I'm a little too busy to show up for this latest dream debut. She knows how I feel."

"That dreams are a waste of time," he said.

Annie nodded. Especially, she added silently, staring at West, when you embellished upon them like she was right now. She was thinking for the first time that hers would really be a dream if *he* were the one to fulfill it.

For a second she wondered if he could read her thoughts, because his dark eyes suddenly lost his weary-old-man look. Now he was staring at her with an intensity that made her wonder if he wanted to kiss her as much as she wanted him to. They gazed at each other for seconds that ticked into eternity, and with all her heart, Annie wished she could give up her dream, or West could give up his pain and his fear of love, and that he *would* kiss her again—and again, and again. But that would be ridiculous…out of the question.…

Idiocy, West thought, breaking the connection between them by pushing himself up off the sofa to get his notebook in the dining room. He wanted badly to kiss Annie again, but that would be lunacy on his part when nothing could ever come of it.

He came back with his notes and sat on the chair on the other side of the coffee table. "It took a while," he told her, "but I finally outlined a plan that will help you achieve what you want."

Two distinct emotions passed over Annie's face— first fear, and then excitement. Her breath caught and her eyes brightened. But then, as though she thought that she were showing him too much of her inner thoughts, she bowed to kiss the sleeping Teddy on the top of his downy-soft head. Rising, she laid him gently down in his playpen. When she finally sat down and faced him again, she was her usual composed self.

"Go ahead, Gallagher," she said too brightly. "I'd love to hear what you've come up with."

"Annie, it's okay. You can let yourself believe." West made a decision right then and there for better or worse—probably for worse—and he told her just so he couldn't take it back. "I'm not going to give up on you until you've got your baby." There, now he'd gone and committed himself to helping her find some man to take her to bed. He must be nuts.

Annie didn't say a word, and he couldn't tell what she was thinking, so there was only one thing left to do—begin. "I've broken your dream down into three major steps."

"I didn't know making a baby was so complicated," she said with a gentle smirk.

"Do you want this or not?" he asked sternly over the top of his notebook.

"Sorry," she said.

"First, you write down your exact dream, focusing on the parts you need to make it come true."

Her smile widened. "Do you mean anatomical parts?"

"No." He scowled, wondering if she were teasing him or making fun of him. There was a difference. "Am I going to have to walk you totally through this?"

"'Fraid so," she said with a nod.

He sighed. "What I mean is, you want first to figure out if you want a real person or a donation."

"Both. I want a real man to donate his side of it."

"Then you want a sperm bank."

"No." She looked flustered, making West wonder how much actual thought she'd given to her plan. But then she continued. "I don't want an anonymous donor. I want to know the father and make sure he's a good man at heart."

She was serious. "That's going to make this that much harder," he told her.

"If it were easy, West, I would have had my baby by now." The thought hung in the air between them for a long moment, and then she rose. "I need a drink of something before we continue," she said. "Want anything?"

He shook his head. As she padded into the next room, West followed with his eyes, watching the swing of her hips in the faded shorts she wore. She'd caught her hair in a long braid down her back, and suddenly he ached to take the golden rope apart and run his fingers through her loose hair.

Her hair, hell. He wanted to run his fingers all over her, touch her everywhere.

Frowning at the direction his thoughts were taking, West moved into the next room and sat down at the dining room table where he'd left the rest of his paper and his pen. Babies and relationships. Never before had they ever been this important—so why now? How in the hell had he ended up with both a baby and a relationship—of sorts—in his own house, rousing him out of his calm solitude? Until the two of them had shown up two days ago, he'd been happy. Now he was…

Involved.

He stared through the hallway into the kitchen, where he could see Annie clinking ice into a glass, and then around to the living room and the sleeping baby in the playpen. The house seemed vibrant now that Annie was back. Warm, full of life.

Maybe he should get a dog.

Annie walked in with a glass of ice tea, grabbed a coaster, and took a seat near him, shooting a skeptical look at his notepad. "Is there a test?"

"The paper is for the parts of your dream," he reminded her. "It's best to write everything down. That way you don't get overwhelmed by thinking the details are insurmountable."

They were insurmountable, Annie thought as West began writing, but she didn't voice that opinion. Instead, she leaned forward until she could see what he had written.

West finished and looked up, right at the view of her cleavage. He gulped. "Maybe I do need a drink."

"'Live donor'?" she asked as he walked to the kitchen. "Does that mean I have to go to bed with him?"

"Him, who?" West asked before he thought, and then he quickly covered his tracks. "Never mind. 'Live donor' is whatever you decide it means." His throat went even drier at the thought she might already have a man in mind for the job. "I'm staying out of that part," he called to her.

"That might be wise," she agreed. "They say three's a crowd."

This was torture. Popping a soda can tab, West got his drink and joined her again. Clearing his throat, he continued. "Okay, we were writing down your dream, focusing on its parts. You want to have the baby and keep your pro bono clients. So that means you need financial and networking support."

Feeling Annie's eyes on him, he talked about looking into having either a partner or hiring secretarial help to handle some of the paperwork so she could handle both her pro bono and her paying cases.

"I had a secretary when I had a partner," she told him.

"You had a partner?" he asked.

"Joel Malcoby," she said, her lips pursing for a second as she remembered. "Malcoby and Robicheaux. He lasted one year until he won three high-profile cases and got wooed away by a downtown legal monopoly. He took my secretary and two of my best clients with him, and along with it, my trust in outsiders. No more partners."

West looked so startled at what she'd told him that Annie almost added, "So there," but instead, she closed her mouth to see what he would say next. She was fascinated that he'd given her dream this much thought. However, he'd merely come up with every solution she had so far, which meant he wasn't going to fish her answers out of the sky.

His eyes were troubled. "If you really want this dream, Annie, you're going to have to learn to trust again."

"Trusting isn't *my* problem."

"Isn't it?"

Now he was getting on her nerves. "Time is my problem. The ticking of the clock. If I had enough time, I would handle all the cases of everyone who needs me, and the cases of the people I need to stay in business—the ones with the thick wallets. But there is never enough time.''

West, as though he wasn't listening, jotted down a few words. ''I've got more thinking to do on the financial end, but rest assured, Annie, I will come up with something.'' He grinned up at her. ''Trust me.''

Trust him. She had to smile back. ''You are the most optimistic so-and-so I have ever met in my whole life, did you know that?''

He grinned wider and rose. ''Now, if you don't mind, I'm ready to hit the sofa. This daddy bit does take its toll.'' Ripping off the top two pages of the notes he'd taken, he handed them to her. ''Embellish on what I've written down for Part One tonight. Come up with some names of prospective fathers. If you don't, I'll be happy to come up with a couple possibilities for you.''

''Do you know anyone who isn't a dreamer?''

''I might surprise you.''

''I believe I'll take care of that part on my own, thank you.'' Annie thought the less West knew about any potential fathers, the less interfering he could do in the future, should he be so inclined. ''But what about Parts Two and Three?''

''Got you interested, huh?''

''You've got me wanting to wring your neck in your sleep,'' she said sweetly from between gritted teeth as she folded the notes and stuck them in her pocket. ''Parts Two and Three, West?''

''You do Part One for me tonight,'' he said, grinning at her scowl, "and I promise I'll give you Part Two tomorrow."

If he seriously believed she was going to hand over to him the names of men she wanted to father her baby, Annie thought, picking up Teddy and heading toward the stairs, tomorrow was going to be one interesting tug-of-war—with her heart right in the middle.

7

Annie's bedtime forecast of Monday with West turned out to be right on target. He *had* believed she was going to come downstairs with a list, and the more he hinted, probed and just plain asked her to produce it, the more she dug in her heels against doing so. And because she wouldn't give him any names, he'd refused to tell her Parts Two and Three of his plan. By late that afternoon, she and West were at a stalemate.

Worse, the three-day bet over who was the better parent to Teddy—and with it her time with West— was about to draw to a close. By mutual agreement, they had decided to have one last meal together outside on the patio before going inside to settle the question of who would keep the baby.

"I've just figured out why you've been so close-mouthed all day," West said.

Having finished the last of her sandwich, Annie glanced over to check on Teddy, who was happily rolling over in his playpen to the side of them, before she looked back at West.

"Okay, know-it-all," she said, "tell me why."

"Because you haven't come up with any possible fathers yet."

"I didn't say that." Flustered, Annie tried not to show it by smiling sweetly at him. How did he read people so well? He was one thin line of notepaper from the truth. "I do have a name—or two, but I think the actual father might be better left on a need-to-know basis."

West considered this for a moment, staring at the window behind Annie's head. They'd left it partially open while they were outside so they could hear the phone ring—or even better, the doorbell. Both of them had been praying Marcia would get an attack of conscience on the holiday and return. At least West was, because pretty soon Annie would be leaving him and he'd be alone with Teddy and real fatherhood.

"A need-to-know basis, huh?" he said. "I hope that includes the father being told."

"Of course." How could West think her without at least that much integrity? "The way I see it, as long as the deed is done, you don't really need to know the particulars of how I have this baby, do you?" Annie paused to take a quick sip of her soda. "You already said you have no personal interest in my having a child. If you're helping me just to prove you aren't a fake, why should you care who the father is?"

"I just want to make sure you have one." West wondered if Annie realized she could talk circles around him. "If you don't, I've made a few friends in the city you might be interested in." West felt total irrational jealousy every time he thought about Annie with another man, but she was right. He had no claim to her, so he shouldn't care whom she had a relationship with.

He shouldn't—but he did. She was so vulnerable. He sensed it in every sweep of her eyelashes, in the way her mouth tilted when she thought about his questions. He didn't want anyone taking advantage of her during her quest to have her child.

Annie didn't bother to reply to West's offer, choosing instead to turn and watch Teddy play as she thought about whose name she *had* written down on the small sheet of paper—West's. The more she'd considered men last night, the better she'd liked the idea of West doing the deed, for various reasons. He had a heart. He was the only man she'd spent any real time with in the past two years. And since he didn't want children, he'd never ask for custody rights, she was sure. And on top of all that, there was the way she felt inside when she looked into those dark eyes of his. Warm, sexy, heated up. Going to bed with West would definitely not be a chore. Every time he looked at her or their skin brushed together, she felt like a woman again, and it had been so long since she'd let herself remember how that felt.

But all that was a fantasy, Annie knew. Her major problem would be convincing West that it wouldn't be the end of the world if she had his offspring and then walked away. And knowing what kind of man he was, changing his already set mind would be impossible—even if she had the time.

"Okay," she said, turning back to West, "let's play it your way. What happens with your plan to help me get my dream if I don't have a father lined up?''

"We go ahead with it," he said, catching her eyes with the twinkle in his. "As I told you last night, I'm sure I can help you out in that department."

If only, she muttered under her breath.

"I'll arrange something."

His comeback had been so quick, for a second or two she thought he'd read her lips. But he was looking innocently back at her, dashing her hopes in that direction.

"Why look for a prospective father if I can't afford the baby anyway? Remember, I can't take on better paying cases and still have time for the people who really need me. I tried that. It didn't work."

She was steering this all back to money again. West gave her a concerned frown. "Surely for something this important, you could compromise a little?"

"I tried compromise." She smiled whimsically. "I took on some bigger clients, and when Marcia needed help, I didn't have time for her. Compromise doesn't work in this case. This experience with Teddy and Marcia has proven to me I can't be happy with people who need me at the bottom of my work pile."

But she wouldn't be happy without having a baby, either, West thought, trying to figure out what was really standing in Annie's way. He didn't think it was only money.

"Have you considered working for something like legal aid to get a steady paycheck?"

"Yes, but then I might end up having to defend

someone who is really guilty of something horrendous. I don't want to do that, either.''

"Hmm" was all he said.

Annie stiffened. "What does that mean?"

"For someone who claims to really want a baby, you seem to be using every possible avenue out of having one you can find."

He said it so gently, Annie didn't think he was trying to make her mad. So that meant only one thing.

"Why, West, are you discovering I was right after all, and there is no solution to my getting what I want?"

"There might be if you weren't so darned stubborn about every detail."

"I thought that was the idea behind having your dream come true."

"Next thing you'll be telling me it's got to be a boy."

She shook her head slowly, her face awash in sadness. "I'd be an equal opportunity mother, West—if it ever happens."

"It will happen," West promised her, unable to stay angry. After what she'd been through in life already, she couldn't help not believing in what he did. She was kind of a lost soul, going through life not having all that she could, and he couldn't abandon her until he helped her get her dream baby. "Even though you're leaving soon, we'll keep meeting until you get your dream. I promise."

Annie felt a rush of some deep feeling go through her insides. This business about dreams might be just so much hype, but West really believed in them. He was so hopeful, when he ought to be jaded—like she was. Admiration for the man and a little bit of envy flooded through her. She'd believe he was a miracle worker if she got her baby, and not a minute before, but there was one thing she was sure of either way.

"West Gallagher, you are one nice guy. But are you still going to be this nice when I win the bet and steal Teddy away from you?"

"You aren't going to win the bet."

"Wanna bet?" she asked cockily.

West's grin came quick and easy, but it also covered his confusion. Now that the time of reckoning was at hand, he didn't know if he wanted her to leave or not.

Annie rose and began gathering things to take inside as West finished the last of his sandwich. When her hands were full, Annie saw that he was done eating and paused.

"What do you say we get this over with, West? Get Teddy inside so we can settle our bet?"

"Sounds good to me," West said, rising. Much as he liked having her there, he needed her to leave so they could have a little distance from each other. When she came out of the kitchen and back to the table, he asked, "So how exactly are we going to figure out who Teddy prefers as a parent?"

Pausing, Annie stared at West for well over a minute, and suddenly she began to grin. "I don't know."

"We're even on the points, you know."

She sincerely hoped so, for every time West had thought of something, not to be outdone, Annie had

snuck a peak at her baby book and found something
else she could get a credit for.

"Let's go inside," she said, walking over to pick
up Teddy. "And we'll figure it out there."

"You go ahead. I'll get the playpen."

Trying to think of some fair way to end this particular dispute, Annie scooped up Teddy and went
inside the kitchen. She was just reaching the door
leading to the hallway when the phone rang behind
her. She sprang for it, hoping it was Marcia and the
question of Teddy, at least, would be settled.

"Gallagher residence," she said, just as Teddy
grabbed for the receiver and started a loud string of
"dadadada" in her ear and the mouthpiece.

"Well, hello," came a feminine voice that held
both surprise and a hint of a chuckle all at once. "I'm
West's sister-in-law, Gina, and I'm just dying to
know why West has a female answering the phone
with a baby yelling 'dada' in his very own house.
Could you put him on, please?"

West was at the door, waiting, his eyebrows raised
hopefully. Annie held out the receiver and smiled.
"You're in trouble. It's your sister-in-law."

"Oh."

"The one who got you those adorable shorts," Annie added, unable to stop herself.

West groaned and took the phone. "How about if
you go outside before you cause any more damage?"

"Sure." She got to the door at the same time he
told Gina hello. There was a short pause, and then
Annie heard West sigh exasperatedly.

"No, Gina, I haven't been hiding a secret family

from you and Matthew. Yes, she's seen the shorts, and no, they didn't do a thing for my love life.''

Annie could say something loudly enough for West's caller to hear…but she decided not to, not yet anyway. West hadn't folded the playpen, so she put Teddy back in it and sat at the patio table where there was no avoiding the one-sided conversation floating through the window. Teddy happily started pushing himself up on all fours, his bright eyes seeking and finding her and not letting go as he babbled a string of unintelligible syllables.

''That was Teddy and Annie. We're baby-sitting,'' West was saying. ''Oh, no, don't worry, I don't need anybody's help with Teddy. Believe me, Annie's been more than enough help.''

He sounded exasperated. Annie's lips pursed together in close to a smile, but before she could worry that she'd put him in a bad mood, her eyes were caught by Teddy. At the sound of West's deep voice, the baby's head had turned to the window. Now Annie watched the baby, her forehead wrinkling as she thought.

''Okay,'' West added, ''put Matt on… Yeah, it's me.'' His voice lowered, but Annie could still hear him. ''Not that it's any of your business, but we aren't. Annie saw the shorts by accident. Did Gina tell you to ask me that?'' West chuckled, but to Annie's ears, the sound seemed grim. ''No, I'm not the baby's father. You can tell your sweet little wife that Annie is just a friend, and we're doing a favor for another friend. I have no interest in being a father, it's that simple. None, absolutely none.''

"You're protesting too much, West," Annie called inside through the window, unable to resist.

West shot her a scowl through the screen. "No, I swear!" he said into the phone. "Annie just has a warped sense of humor. By the end of the week the baby will be back with its mama, and I'll return to being the happy bachelor again." There was quiet, and West spoke again, sounding worried. "You know I would love to see you and Gina, but it's not a good time."

Not a good time to see the brother he'd only recently reunited with? Why on earth not? Pondering that one, Annie glanced back at the baby, and saw that the child had given up trying to crawl and was now looking intently in the direction of West's voice.

"Teddy," she called. The baby's head swiveled to her, and he let out another stream of syllables.

She got up and as she bent over and picked up the baby, she got her idea. Maybe there was a way to figure out who would be the winner of the bet. If it worked, it sure would be interesting to see whom Teddy picked.

"Thank you, Annie," West said from the door. Walking over to the playpen, he began gathering up the padding. "Do you know how much trouble you got me into with your little remark about protesting too much? Gina wanted to come here and plan the wedding."

"Did you tell them we were making a baby first?" she teased, her mouth opening in a wide smile.

"*We* are not making a baby," he reminded her.

"Well, technically, if you're helping me figure out my dream, then we are."

His jaw set, he straightened, glaring fiercely at her. She held back a giggle. "Okay, West, whatever you say."

After a long look at her, West gathered up the rest of the playpen padding and disappeared into the house, coming back a minute later to unhitch the pen. He was glad Matt and Gina weren't coming. He didn't need any questions about Teddy—or about Annie. It had been hard enough to evade the particulars of his current situation over the phone. Face-to-face, he was sure he'd end up telling his brother and Gina all about this whole lost weekend, and then he'd never hear the end of it. Matt with teasing, and Gina with wanting to help him, because all his sister-in-law would have to do would be take one look at him and Annie, and she'd know West had lied about Annie just being a friend.

For damned sure. He took a deep breath. The depth of his desire to pull Annie into his arms and kiss that know-it-all look off her face a minute before meant their relationship had already surpassed simple friendship—at least for him. Even now, he wanted to tell Annie she was right about him, that he couldn't make her dream come true, and that he didn't want to settle their bet, because he wanted her to stay right where she was—with him. He liked her. Not only did he admire what she wanted to do with her life—fatherless baby notwithstanding—he liked the courage she showed standing up to him and her willingness to fight for what she believed in.

And God knew, he wanted her in his bed. But if he convinced her to stay with him and build a relationship without children, she'd end up hating him. And he couldn't have it the other way, in case it didn't work out between them. He couldn't do that to their child, and he couldn't be ripped away from love again.

Women, he muttered under his breath, carrying the playpen into the house. The second you let them into your life, everything got too damned complicated.

Silently, Annie entered the living room and sat on the couch with the baby. West watched as he set up the playpen in the corner. Now that he knew she would be leaving, he remained aware of her every movement, her every sigh, even the sound of when she kissed Teddy. She was driving him crazy, and he'd be a damned fool to let her stay.

And he'd be a damned fool if he let her go. But he had to, so he didn't end up breaking her heart— and his own.

Done with the playpen, West stood, remaining well away from her. "Did you come up with any ideas?"

Annie read hope in his eyes—he wanted to get rid of her. "As a matter of fact…I did. While I wasn't here, have you called Teddy's name and had him lift his arms up to you, wanting to be picked up?"

West nodded.

"So have I." She took a deep breath. "This whole bet was based on who would be the better parent, and who Teddy would prefer—a man or a woman, you or me—to take care of him, right?"

"Right."

"I'm proposing we sit Teddy on the floor and each sit an equal distance to either side of him. Then we call his name from either side until he turns toward one of us and shows a definite preference—let's say by putting his arms out to be picked up. How about that?"

He'd feel silly as hell, West thought, like he was in one of those ultra-sweet baby commercials. But he couldn't think of any other way to end the bet. And every second he was in the room with Annie, smelling the rose of her perfume, he wanted to take her in his arms even more. He had to get some distance.

He ought to just let her have the baby. She wasn't going to turn Teddy in, he was sure of that now. She'd already said she felt she failed Marcia; she wouldn't do it again by giving her baby to the authorities. Teddy was safe with Annie—West knew it in his gut—but for some reason, he just couldn't let the kid go. Not yet. He didn't want to face the empty house without him.

"Sounds as good as anything," West said finally. "Where?"

"The hallway?" West had vacuumed earlier that day, so Annie knew the rug was clean. "No distractions," she said, her mouth twisting with bittersweet mirth as she saw that Teddy's attention was not focused on them at the moment, but on the crystal chandelier West had turned on when they'd come into the room.

"Lead the way." Following Annie and the baby into the hall, West waited as she sat Teddy down and went to the opposite side of him, about two feet away.

Copying her position, he sat down and spread his legs into a vee.

Let the games begin, fluttered through West's mind, and he almost grinned.

"Teddy," they both said at practically the same time.

Caught in the middle of both sounds, Teddy looked first at Annie, and then turned his head and looked at West. Annie's breath caught as the baby seemed to stare at West longer, and she repeated his name again, just as West was doing.

Teddy heard her and turned his head away from West toward Annie. West, watching, felt his heart sink as Teddy began to babble at Annie in absolute delight. The baby was going to her, he knew it.

Slowly, Teddy rolled over on to his tummy, and then rose on to his hands and knees. Both Annie and West called his name one more time, and he began to creep along, carefully at first and then with more energy—right toward West.

"He's crawling!" Annie said, gulping back her sadness at the fact that Teddy was heading toward West, which meant she would not be needed here anymore. She caught West's eyes. "Did you know he could do that?"

Shaking his head, West thought of how he had believed Annie silly for putting all those pillows on his bed as a guard for Teddy each night, and swallowed hard. What if Teddy had started crawling in the middle of the night and fallen off?

"He is, isn't he?" he said.

Teddy was. The baby was crawling, slowly but

surely, West noted, right up toward him…and then right on past, until he reached the doorway leading back into the living room, where he gave out and fell to his tummy, flapped his arms and legs, and let out a stream of happy babbling. Still mesmerized by the sight of Teddy doing something for the first time, Annie rose and hurried to where Teddy had landed.

She squatted next to West. ''I don't understand,'' she said. ''I thought he was crawling to you.''

''I thought he was, too.''

''So what's so interesting in there?''

They both leaned forward toward the doorway at the same time, and West found himself perilously close to Annie, who had stooped down on her knees. So close his upper arm brushed against hers, skin against skin, sending shock waves through him and making his body jerk with reaction. He pulled away a bit and she rearranged herself in the doorway, sitting and pulling Teddy backward onto her lap. In doing so, she brushed against West, more than once, and then her hip settled against his thigh.

He caught a groan in his throat, remembering the way her legs had looked in stockings. This was torture—and he wasn't sure he wanted it to end.

''He really crawled,'' Annie said again. ''Isn't this great?'' Her eyes lit up as she gazed at West, and he couldn't stop himself.

''Wonderful,'' he repeated, not knowing whether he really meant Teddy's crawling—or Annie. Leaning sideways and balancing on one arm, he met her lips in a tender kiss that took her by surprise, because she'd thought they were ending, not beginning.

Annie's skin began to tingle as West's lips lingered against hers, touching gently, then pressing more firmly. Her breath caught in her throat and her heart began a strange beat. All at once she was again remembering West's power, and wondered what it would be like to make love with him.

The kiss ended when Teddy wiggled downward to the floor, plopped forward and began crawling again with a little more self-assurance than he'd shown before. Sitting himself down mere inches in front of Annie, he looked upward, and Annie and West followed the direction of his gaze.

"The chandelier?" West asked.

"No," Annie said softly, lifting her hand and pointing to the wall. "I think Teddy found a rainbow."

"It figures," West said, his voice a mixture of wry amusement. "We set up a bet, knock ourselves out for the kid for three days, and what does Teddy prefer to either of us? A rainbow."

"Maybe he's trying to find the bright spot in all of this," Annie said, meeting his eyes.

Both of them started laughing, and West got the strangest feeling it was somehow right that Teddy had ignored them for the lure of a rainbow, that for some reason, they weren't supposed to end the bet tonight. The three of them were meant to stay together until Teddy went home. The more he considered it, the more right the idea felt.

Their laughter had once again caught the baby's attention, and forgetting the rainbow of lights the chandelier cast, Teddy twisted and held out his arms to West.

"Now he wants me," West groaned. "Story of my life. Nobody ever wants me until it's too late."

Annie's heart skipped a beat. She wished she could tell him how much she wanted him now, but she couldn't. He might think her desire meant she was willing to give up her dream for him, and how could she do that? The past few days with Teddy had fanned the spark into a full-blown fire again.

She couldn't say a word, and didn't, but as he looked from Teddy up to her, and they gazed at each other for a long minute, there was a look in his eyes that said he wanted her there, and he was going to ask her to—

"Stay," he said, as though some magic had overtaken the two of them and they were reading each other's thoughts. "Please stay, Annie. I meant what I said. It takes two people to make a child happy, and until Marcia comes back, we're all Teddy's got. I can't give him up, and I don't think you can, either."

Annie still didn't know what to do. Thinking it out, she rose, took Teddy, and carried him back to the playpen.

Even as West's common sense told him having Annie in the same house with him five more days was going to be hell, something else inside of him was making him say, "C'mon, Annie, it's a good idea."

Getting his mouth wired shut right now would be a good idea, too, he thought, but it was too late for that.

"I don't know, West." A part of her wanted to

remain, but another part of her was afraid of the attraction she was feeling toward West, both physical and mental. It was magnified now—what would it be like by Saturday? And what if Marcia didn't come back like she promised? She could end up living here for a while, falling in love with a man who never wanted a wife or children.

It would never work out between them.

"Look," West said, rising to face her, "we're better as a team, right here. It's not good for Teddy to be moved again, but even if you took him home, you'd need to investigate sitters, and that takes time. How are you going to handle him alone? And if he stays here with me, I've got the same problem. This way, we're together enough to coordinate schedules without running around, and we can still work on your dream."

Her dream, Annie thought. A baby, a family, her career. Through some perversity, she was living it as they spoke—only this version had a man in it. Maybe somewhere out there another woman was short one man in hers. She looked up at West speculatively. Uh-uh. She wasn't giving him back. Not yet, anyway.

"It'll work out. Everything will," West said, without believing it himself. As sure as he knew he couldn't let her leave just yet, he also knew one or both of them was going to end up getting hurt. He'd better make damned sure it was him in the end. He could handle it. He could handle anything.

It was the motto he lived by.

"All right, West," Annie said slowly. "I'll stay."

8

As Annie came down the stairs the next evening dressed to attend Gigi's debut, West's breath caught, and he cursed himself for the mistake of his life he was about to make. Annie wore a floral print dress that emphasized her delicacy and outlined every curve of her hips and small waist. As if its plunging neckline filled with white lace wasn't enough to choke him, the dress buttoned down the front and the bottom two buttons were open. With every step Annie took, her thigh played peekaboo.

She'd obviously picked the dress to torture him, and she didn't even have a good reason—yet.

''You aren't dressed up,'' Annie said when she reached the bottom of the steps and saw West still in his jeans and sport shirt. He couldn't be attending Gigi's debut dressed like that—which meant he didn't plan to go at all. One look into his deep blue eyes verified it.

''If you didn't want to go, West, why on earth didn't you just say so?'' Shards of disappointment cut through her. She'd thought he cared, that he'd be there to help her bolster up Gigi if her aunt flopped.

"The baby-sitter canceled." Actually, West had called Gigi's friend Miss Grinzy and told her not to come, that he had made other plans for Teddy that evening—which was true. Keeping in mind that he was supposed to be distancing himself from Annie while she was in his home, he'd decided a romantic evening at a bistro with Annie was out of the question. But since Annie still needed to go, he thought he would help her out with her dream by arranging her date to be with husband material…and he'd found her just the man.

"But don't worry," he told her, pulling at his collar, which suddenly seemed too tight, "you aren't going alone."

Annie's mouth twisted. "I hope that means you have a clone."

"Some people think we're equally good-looking." The doorbell rang and, grinning, West hurried to answer it. By the goofy, pleased grin on his face, Annie thought, apparently he was no longer worried about women leaving babies on his doorstep.

She paused in the living room doorway as he opened the front door. No baby this time. This time his visitor was a man—one right off the cover of *GQ*.

"C'mon in, Rome," West said. "I want you to meet Annie, your date for the evening. Annie, this is Rome. He's a cop," he added, shading his voice with a barely perceptible warning.

With a rush of suddenness, Annie realized two things. First, Miss Grinzy hadn't canceled, she'd *gotten* canceled, and second, Rome was there on purpose. He was part of West's plan.

Rome was a potential daddy.

Clamping her lips shut, Annie extended her hand with a tight smile and, as they shook, said in one breath, "I'm pleased to meet you." Pause. "West, we have to talk in the kitchen."

West looked reluctant. "But you two are going to be late if you waste any time—"

"Now," she said over her shoulder, already half-way through the living room.

"Arguing with me," West finished. He shot Roman Markham a lame smile—what could he do?—and followed Annie, closing the kitchen door so they wouldn't be overheard.

"Rome?" Annie asked in a quiet, rushed voice, her eyes bright with irritation. "You're sending me out into the dark night on a romantic date with a guy who looks like a male model, but who is really a tall, dark and handsome cop named *Rome?"*

"Did you want a blond?" West asked. "Because if you want a blond, we're in trouble. I don't have any blond friends."

"I don't believe you." Annie gave him her iciest stare. "I thought you didn't trust cops."

"I don't trust the system," West said, very serious about that. "But as far as his dating you goes, you're old enough to take care of yourself. Besides, Rome is a nice enough guy—" Stopping, he pretended to reconsider. "But then again, Annie, maybe I should warn him about *you.*"

"Gee, thanks."

He grinned. "He should be perfect for what you want. He's not into attachments, and you want him to leave you alone after the deed is done, don't you? His gene pool seems okay. He's smart, and you just said he's good-looking.''

Annie whooshed out a breath to calm down. West was only trying to help, but his choosing the father of her baby felt too odd, so she fished around for an excuse for him to get rid of Rome.

''I don't trust great-looking men,'' she said. *There.*

''You trust me, don't you?'' West asked with a twinkle in his eye.

''Why of course, West,'' she said smoothly. When his face fell into a frown, she smiled wickedly. ''Gotcha. I told you not to arrange dates for me.''

''Like I said—'' His eyes grazed over her with a potent look of concentration that made her shiver. ''You can take care of yourself. So tell me why you really don't want to give Rome a chance.''

Annie's hazel eyes glanced toward the door. ''I don't know.'' But she did. She'd set her heart on West and he was already throwing her to the wolves. ''Am I safe with Rome?''

''He's a *cop,*'' West reminded her in a hushed voice.

She made a sound that resembled a groan. ''How long have you known him?''

''He sold me this house, and we've been friends ever since.'' West grabbed her shoulders firmly enough that she looked him straight in the eyes. ''Are you sure you want this dream of yours?''

Feeling the heat of his hands through the thin sleeves of her dress, Annie's insides began turning cartwheels and she couldn't answer him at first. "Yes," she said finally.

"Yes, what?"

"Yes, I want this dream. Only…" She knew she shouldn't say this, but she couldn't stop herself. "Only maybe you should know before I agree to this date. There *is* a name on the list of possible fathers you told me to write down, West."

"Who?" West asked, filled with dread. Another date he'd have to suffer through.

"You," she whispered, her hazel eyes huge. "I wish it could be you."

West swallowed, feeling the loss of her in every part of his body, especially his heart. "I wish it could be, too, Annie, but I can't change what's deep inside me."

"Can't, or won't?"

"Can't," he said firmly. "Could you give up your dream of having a baby and still be happy?"

She hesitated for so long, West's hope grew, but then she shook her head. "All right," she said. "You win. I'll give Rome a shot." Squaring her shoulders, she gave West a brave grin, turned and headed toward the kitchen door. "Wish me luck."

Luck—in what? Figuring out what, West double-stepped to catch up with her. "How about two shots?" he asked, close to her ear so Rome couldn't hear. "I mean, you're not going to try anything on the first date, are you? Should I warn him?"

"West," she scolded, shaking her head at him. "You created this monster, now you're going to have to live with it. And I don't kiss and tell." With a wiggle-wave of her fingers that reminded West of her aunt Gigi, she pushed through the kitchen door, leaving West behind.

Had he made a mistake? West wondered. Surely she wouldn't jump into bed with Rome just to get it over with tonight, would she? She wasn't *that* desperate to get her dream started, was she?

Hell.

Teddy let out a wail, barring West from further speculation, and swearing under his breath, he hurried into the living room. Annie was picking up Teddy as he came in, cooing to him to get him to calm down.

Rome was standing by the sofa, nervously shifting his weight from foot to foot. ''I'm sorry if I scared him,'' he said, shoving back the dark lanks of hair that had fallen onto his forehead. ''All I did was come into the room when I saw Annie. Whose baby is it?''

''He's my nephew,'' West lied before Rome asked any more questions. He couldn't tell him about the baby in the basket, just in case Rome ceased being a friend and remembered he was part of the system. All Rome knew was that Annie was his friend and needed an escort to her aunt's singing debut. ''You two go along,'' West added, taking Teddy from Annie. ''He'll be fine. You know where the Café Lauree is, right, Rome?''

''I sure do,'' Rome said over Teddy's wails, holding out his arm for Annie, his handsome face serious. ''You look lovely, Annie.''

''I appreciate your saying so,'' Annie replied, batting her eyelashes just to make West mad.

It worked. Pangs of jealousy hit West with the sting

of shotgun pellets as he rocked Teddy, and he told himself to be strong. This was what both he and Annie wanted. Yeah, right. Like he wanted a baby on his doorstep, he wanted Annie smiling that gentle smile of hers at Rome.

Annie caught West's scowl and purposely kissed Teddy and reached up to pat West's cheek. "You two have fun. I will."

As soon as the door closed, West knew he wasn't going to have any such thing. What he was going to do was spend the entire evening being miserable.

Annie was obsessing, and she couldn't stop herself. Her aunt Gigi was beside the piano in the Café Lauree, talking to the pianist before starting her final song. Rome had been wonderfully attentive and polite—if a little serious and reserved for her tastes—but all Annie could think about was West. No matter how good his intentions had been, how dare he pull a last-minute date switch on her! She set her lips tightly. She hoped her parting remarks had left him worrying all evening.

Glancing around the café, Annie drank in the atmosphere of the newest hot spot in the city. Located on the outskirts of the French Quarter, it was minutes away from the market, Bourbon Street, and all the other attractions that made New Orleans so touristy popular. Aunt Gigi had called it a bistro, but it was really a nightclub with food. The menu was limited, but the seafood had been excellent. With its well-dressed waiters and the piano player, the place actually had charm that provided a beautiful backdrop for the night's star attraction, Gigi, glowing in her shimmering turquoise gown.

The haunting strains of the love ballad Gigi started singing drew Annie's attention back to her aunt. Not only was Gigi's voice lovely, this song was beautiful, about love lost and never rekindled being as soft and fragile as butterfly wings. Annie had never heard it anywhere before, and as Gigi finished the number, she wondered if her aunt had written it.

It didn't matter if she had or hadn't, Gigi was a success, and Annie joined wholeheartedly in the applause, tears of joy in her eyes. Her tears came with happiness—for both her aunt and herself. West had been right after all. Dreams *were* obtainable. Oh, she was no fool—Gigi changed dreams like she changed her hairstyle, regularly, according to whim. But all her aunt's "dreams"—designing, painting, acting, and now singing—had pointed to one thing: Gigi wanted to be noticed and admired. From the enthusiastic way people were clapping, it looked like Gigi had somehow finally settled on the right way to make that dream come true.

"She's seen us," Annie said to Rome as Gigi made her way through the crowd toward them. Both she and Rome stood to congratulate her.

"My *petite* babee, you came!"

Hearing the accent, Rome looked at Annie. "She's from France?"

"Everyone thinks that," Annie said, and then opened her arms. "Aunt Gigi, I'm so proud of you!"

Flushed with happiness, Gigi hugged Annie against her ample bosom and backed away, gazing at Rome.

"We will talk of my success in a minute. For right now, I must know—who ees your handsome man, and what did you do with West Gallagher?"

Annie introduced Rome as her date. "And to answer your second question," she told Gigi, "I didn't do anything to West." Not that I don't plan to later, she added silently. "He's at home baby-sitting Teddy."

"And so the bet has ended, and you are not living—"

"Excuse me," Annie said to Rome, smiling at him as she spirited Gigi away to a less populated spot near the kitchen, where they'd be interrupted only by an occasional waiter. Giving her a thumbnail version of the newest developments, including that West was helping her with her dream of having a baby, she concluded, "West and Rome are friends, Aunt Gigi, but Rome is a cop. Since West didn't want him to know the truth about Teddy in case Rome had to act on it, he lied to him."

"Aha! So the man you are in love with sent you out to ooh-la-la with his friend? I'm intrigued."

"I am not in love with West," Annie said indignantly.

"Then why are you still there? West can matchmake on the telephone."

"We're just staying together until we can return Marcia's baby," she said softly. "I can't abandon Teddy."

Gigi sniffed. "Malarkey," she scoffed, every trace of her accent gone as tended to happen whenever she got serious. "That man can take care of that baby as well as you can."

"I know," Annie said morosely. "I'm not myself, Aunt Gigi. Living with West has totally racked me. I don't know what I'm saying anymore."

"Sounds like love to me," Gigi said, her eyes twinkling.

Was it? No, it couldn't be—could it? Annie shook her head in denial.

"Fine, fine." Gigi waved her hands as if she didn't care to argue the point. "Just know that West Gallagher is wonderful." She threw her arms out expansively. "This—all of this—I owe to his book. You should reread it, Annie. He made me look deep into myself for the desire I've been denying because I was afraid it would never come true—and suddenly, I knew. I just knew. I said I wanted to sing, but I was too afraid to audition, for fear everyone would laugh. West's words gave me the courage to finally go for it.

"But never mind about me." Oblivious to the hubbub around her, Gigi enveloped Annie in a warm hug and then planted a kiss on her cheek. "If you think this Rome will get you what you want, go for it," she said generously. "As always, I will be happy for you. But please, think about what I've said, and in the end, remember your dream—and follow your heart."

Shooing Annie away, Gigi promptly disappeared to change gowns for her second set, leaving Annie to return to Rome and speculate. What did she really want to do? She ought to be jumping at this oppor-

tunity West had given her to cultivate a father for her
child, but she couldn't think of a thing to say to
Rome. She wouldn't be having that problem with
West—he always had something to say to her. West
cared.

West cared strongly, with every fiber of his being.

The realization made her shiver. She'd been wrong.
West really did care about people. Why else would
he have taken in Teddy, the son of someone he barely
knew? Because he had a heart.

And now he had changed Gigi. Her aunt had finally
figured out her real dream—the thing that would
make her happy—was not what she'd supposed at all.
It had been what she had been most afraid she would
never be able to have.

Gigi had told her to think about that. Could she be
after the wrong thing? And what was she most afraid
she'd never have, and therefore had been avoiding to
keep from being hurt?

Annie knew. Oh, she didn't want to admit it, but
she knew. After Jean-Pierre had destroyed her trust,
she had been closing herself off from men, too afraid
of being hurt to trust in love again. But now she'd
trusted a man enough to open up her heart to him and
tell him that she'd always wanted a child. That had
never happened before, not even with Jean-Pierre.

She took a deep breath. Did she have the courage
to stop circumventing her real dream of being in love
again? Should she be seeking love first—with West,
the only man she trusted and wanted—and pray that
the child naturally followed? What if she were

wrong? And what if loving West turned out to be not enough for her?

"Well, would you look at that?" Rome said, touching her shoulder and waving his hand in the direction of the door. Jerked out of her troublesome thoughts, Annie focused on her surroundings, and what she saw made her mouth drop open.

As West wove his way through the tables, the maître d' close on his heels protesting that babies weren't allowed in the Café Lauree, he saw Annie's change of expression. She was seated very close to Rome on the curved padded seat, the two of them cozy, and she didn't look happy to see him.

Well, fine. West hadn't had that great a time himself this evening, pacing back and forth wearing a permanent path in his carpet while Teddy played happily in his playpen. He had finally admitted to himself he'd made a mistake switching dates on Annie. A huge mistake.

All he could think about was Annie in Rome's arms. He had sent a woman he desperately wanted off with someone perfectly capable of sweeping her off her feet. He knew Rome was lonely—and he knew Annie was vulnerable. What he didn't know—and what was killing him—was, would that combination end them up in bed together the first time she'd met him?

He hadn't been able to wait around until tomorrow to find out. All his life he'd pursued his dreams, and now his dream was having Annie for his own. It might be a dream he could never have, but he'd be damned if he was going to be the one to push her into another man's arms. So he'd grabbed up Teddy, thankful the child had still been awake, and come here to make a spectacle of himself, risking everything he'd worked for if people asked real questions, just in the name of…what? Ruining Annie's dream?

He'd lost his mind.

But he wasn't leaving.

Reaching Annie's table, feeling hopeful and crazy at the same time, West held Teddy well away, snuffed out the candle on the table, and then handed the baby to her. "Teddy missed you," he said.

Teddy took one look at Rome and, just like earlier in the house, burst into a loud wail that would have had everyone in the place's head turning, had they all not been already captivated by the scene.

"Poor baby," Annie crooned. "Are you having a rough evening?"

West suppressed his grin.

"Really, sir," the maître d' broke in stiffly from behind West. "We do not have the facilities for children. And you aren't wearing a tie. We insist on a tie. You'll have to go."

"That's all right, Nigel," Annie told her aunt's new friend, cradling Teddy to her. "We're leaving."

"We are?" Rome asked.

"We are?" West said. He hadn't even had to beg.

"Of course. Teddy so obviously needs me." Rising, Annie handed the baby back to West as she picked up her purse and smiled at Rome. "I'm sorry about this. Thank you for escorting me. I *really* enjoyed myself."

"That much?" West asked.

She turned to West and gave him a long once-over. "That much and *more*." Especially, she'd enjoyed learning her aunt's lesson.

Rome looked from Annie to West, his dark eyes speculative, and then, for the first time since he'd arrived that evening, he actually grinned. "Oh. I see how it is."

"How what is?" West asked.

"Sirs, really," the maître d' piped in, sensing no movement toward the door. "I need that baby off the premises. You wouldn't want me to contact authorities, would you?"

Rome grinned again and started laughing. "No, we wouldn't want you to have to do that." Shaking his dark head in total amusement, he said goodbye. "Call me when you find out how this turns out," he said as he left them.

"We will," Annie called sweetly. She'd seen through West's story the second the happy-looking Teddy had spotted Rome and let out a squall. West had been counting on him not liking Rome as a cover, so he could break things up. It had been West who'd had second thoughts about her being out and begun to suffer.

Knowing that West felt that deeply for her gave her courage to try it West's way—at least the way Aunt Gigi had read it in his book. Instead of a baby, Annie decided, she would go after love. West's love. And if her love for him was powerful and real enough, maybe, just maybe, it could melt the reserve in West's heart and change him so that he would trust her not to leave him. She didn't fear a forever with him—unless he failed to love her. A baby remained a dream in her heart, but she knew she no longer wanted that child unless it had West and forever attached to it.

And if he trusted her, she hoped he would give her that baby. But she would never know unless she gave love a chance without any expectations. She'd never know unless she chanced getting hurt again.

Tonight, with West.

By the time the two of them stopped at a Quik-Shop store so Annie could dash inside for what she termed ''supplies'' and then got home, Teddy was sound asleep.

''So confess, West,'' Annie said as West put the baby down in his padded playpen. ''Was Teddy having the rough evening—or were you?'' Collapsing on the sofa, Annie kicked off her shoes, curled her legs up underneath her, and patted the seat next to her.

''Caught me. I got to thinking about Rome,'' he said, sitting next to her, ''and I decided I was wrong to set him up.'' And jealous as hell, he added silently.

''Rome was safe,'' Annie told him. ''I spent the whole evening comparing him to you.'' She took a deep breath. She could still feel it, this desire entwining her with West, an attraction that had started and grown since she'd first set eyes on him. ''More happened tonight than just Aunt Gigi's success. She told me something interesting, West—that she owes all her success to you. She said I should examine my real dream, just like you say to in the book.''

If there was one thing that was worrying West about having written that book, it was that people were putting a lot of bizarre interpretations on what was in it, like Marcia thinking he'd implied it was okay to abandon her baby. "What precisely did Gigi say I said about real dreams in the book?"

"That what I really want is probably what I fear having the most."

"Oh." He gave Annie a strange look. "So what do you fear the most, Annie?"

"Love." Now that she'd admitted it, she wanted to get everything out, so she spoke in a rush. "I'm afraid I'll fall in love and get hurt all over again. After Gigi said that, I realized that's why I was so adamant about having a baby alone. It wasn't interference from the father, it was being tied again to a man who didn't love me."

"Oh, hell, Annie," West uttered. She was tearing him apart.

"And since we seem to have these...*feelings*... passing back and forth between us like electric currents, I thought I could go ahead and change my dream to pursuing real, true love—with you." *Only with you.* "That is, if you're willing. And if it's real, true love we end up feeling, maybe the rest about the baby will just fall into place, eventually..."

"I can't promise you that ever, Annie."

"I know." She reached up and stroked her fingers down the side of his clean-shaven cheek and let them rest on his shoulder. "But at least we would have tried. And if it turns out there is love between us, I think we'll end up happy with whatever happens, don't you?''

West didn't know. He wasn't sure he believed in love, and that was part of the problem of having a child. ''You really believe in that kind of love, Annie?''

''Oh, yes,'' she said, nodding solemnly. ''I have to, West—or what's the sense of existing?'' Her hand moved from his shoulder down his chest, more slowly than West had imagined possible, until she reached his belt, where her fingers lingered. Just when he thought he couldn't stand the torment a second longer, Annie dropped her hand to the couch pillow.

''Real love does exist, West, and it's the kind I want—the kind that shines in your eyes when you look at your spouse. The kind that makes everyone else envious, because they know how hard it is to find and keep. The kind where there's a connection of the hearts.''

West had only seen that kind once, when his brother Matthew had looked at his wife during the marriage ceremony. ''So you think we could feel that?''

''We aren't going to ever find out unless we try.'' Annie's smile looked dazzlingly bright to West. ''Unless, of course, you don't want me.''

''If that's a joke…'' he said, wrapping his arms around her and lifting her onto his lap, where she could feel the evidence of just how much he did want her. ''It's a damned poor one.''

He kissed her, his tongue flickering against hers until Annie felt senseless with delight—but not so much that she couldn't pluck free his buttons. Her hand slipped under his shirt and she touched him, explored him, feeling like she was finally free to play with a gift that had been dangled in front of her eyes for days.

Long days.

West continued to kiss her while freeing the pearl buttons on the front of her dress that had kept him hot and bothered the whole time she'd been out with Rome. The lacy piece that covered her cleavage turned out to be a camisole with lace straps.

He loved lace.

Teddy sighed in his sleep, and the noise was like an explosion in the otherwise still room. Annie pulled back, drawing in a deep breath.

"Upstairs," she whispered. "We can't do anything right *here,*" she said, indicating the baby with a sideways sweep of her head. Her hair fell over one shoulder. Seeing it, desire propelled him to his feet, and he watched as Annie quickly checked Teddy in the soft lamplight to make sure he was sound asleep. He was. Then she stopped by her purse and lifted out one of the foil-wrapped condoms she bought earlier at the Quik-Shop. Silently she walked over to him, picked up his hand, and folded his fingers over it. "It's my promise to you that I won't ask you for more than you can give me," she said, smiling up at him.

West didn't know what to say. Annie would voluntarily give up her most heartfelt desire—for him— and that was more than anyone had ever offered him. He could deny his need for her until hell froze over, but if he didn't at least try a relationship with her, he knew he would forever feel like he'd missed a chance at happiness.

But still, he worried about her. "Will my love be enough for you, Annie?"

Annie smiled at him from the bottom of her heart. "If it's real love, West, I believe it will." She batted him gently on the arm, rushed ahead of him and laughed delightedly. "Now hurry up with that thing before I start thinking you're all talk and no action."

"Which thing?" he joked, and then pretended to chase her up the stairs. When they reached the top he caught her around the waist and lifted her up in the air, covering her mouth with his again.

His very size made her feel safe with him, cherished. Annie curled her arms around his neck and returned his kiss. As his tongue probed her mouth, her insides dissolved and she pressed her breasts harder against his chest, needing to assuage the aching want in them. He let her slide down his body until her feet hit the ground in a move that left her panting with need. As if by mutual consent, they both began to strip off their clothes.

Annie, her lips swollen from his kisses and her hazel eyes lit with an inner fire, was every bit as beautiful as West had imagined wearing nothing but her camisole and matching lace panties.

"I am one lucky man," he uttered.

"What's luck got to do with it?" Annie's eyes twinkled as she gazed at West in his dark blue boxer shorts and no shirt. He was magnificent, with shoulders and arms and rippling muscles. "I hope I'm one of your dreams you made come true."

"God, I'm glad I wrote that book," he said, meaning it with all his heart as he pulled her against him again, lowering his mouth back down on hers. He was even a little glad Marcia'd had her lapse of sanity. If she hadn't, he never would have met Annie. He'd never felt this intensity toward a woman before, like he wanted to savor every moment with her at the same time he wanted to devour and be devoured.

As quickly as possible.

They stayed where they were, within seconds caught up in an explosion of flames too hot to let them walk even a couple dozen feet to a bed. Running his hands over her lace-covered breasts and then under them, lifting them, caressing their hardened peaks through the thin material, West acquainted himself with their feel at the same time he gave her pleasure. She moaned and, with a gentle tug on his shoulders, brought him down to the thickly carpeted floor right there with her.

On the floor they kissed, touched and loved each other into a sweet oblivion, and by the time they were totally naked and West made real love to her, Annie was on the edge of ecstasy—and on the edge of falling in love.

Long minutes later, as she lay in West's arms, she couldn't help but think the two of them were perfect for each other and could have that romantic forever they both wanted—if her love could just melt the reserve around West's heart. And if it couldn't, she knew what she was feeling for him was going to be tested. For, more than ever now, she wanted a baby.

West's baby.

9

So much time was taken up on Wednesday juggling baby-watching, her work, and her court schedule, that the day had flown by without Annie seeing much of West. But Wednesday night, falling asleep in his arms after making love had been like finding the pot of gold at the end of Teddy's rainbow, right there in the house—only better. Money never lasted. She really believed love could.

Yawning, she padded barefoot back to West's bed Thursday morning after checking on Teddy in his playpen bed across the hall. He was still asleep. Since it was already daylight and she had only a few minutes until she had to get up anyway, she propped herself up in a sitting position against the pillow-lined headboard and looked down at the man she was ninety-nine percent certain she was in love with.

From when they'd fallen asleep holding each other, she knew West was naked underneath the sheet that half covered him. After studying him for a few seconds to make certain he was still asleep—he seemed to be—she grinned. Unable to resist, she stretched out her leg and used her bare toes to lift up the sheet, getting a good view of his private assets. Still grinning, she crept her other foot stealthily forward and let her toes tickle him to attention, sighing with contentment at the feel of his velvety soft, hot skin.

Before she had time to squeal, West flipped around, grabbed her hips, and slid her down onto her back. Leaning down, he kissed the inside of her thigh above her knee.

"Oh, West," she said, melting inside. "We don't have any time for this. I have an eight-thirty appointment."

"Call and tell them something came up," he said, moving slightly so her hand touched exactly what that something was.

"Something big, huh, West?" she asked, giggling and then gasping for breath as his mouth wandered higher on her sensitive inner thigh.

"And getting bigger," he told her, reaching the bottom of the oversize T-shirt she had worn to bed. He lifted it and continued to kiss a line up her hipbone. "But still not too big for you to handle," he added.

"I guess…I could…try to squeeze you in, then," she said, finding it hard to breathe as he reached her breasts and lowered his mouth directly over one taut peak. "But it's going to be hard."

"I hope so," he said, moving up to kiss her lips as he moved over her and ground his pelvis against hers. Annie's whole body shuddered with anticipation and from that point on, time no longer seemed so important to her. Only West did. Very soon they were going to give Teddy back, and then it would be just the two of them. She had a feeling that she would know then whether or not West felt like she did—that she wanted them to be together forever.

So while she still could, she made love to him and tried not to think about what Saturday would bring. But still the lovemaking was bittersweet, because when they dissolved against each other, finally satiated, the air was thick with her hope and his silence. He still hadn't said how he felt about her or their relationship, and the clock was ticking toward the final hours.

Even though it wasn't very loud, the phone jarred them both; Annie felt West physically startle. Groaning, he remained where he was on top of her because she held him there and reached out with one arm to grab the phone.

"It's seven-thirty in the morning, you're disturbing me, and this better be good," he muttered into the phone without saying hello.

Annie could hear a masculine voice, and she tried to roll away so he could talk, but West held her where she was and shook his head, his eyes going darkly serious. "That's a good one." A long pause, and then dotted conversation. "Yeah, I am… Sure… Oh, no, I'll go to them—it would be easier… Yeah, I'm positive. I know where that is… In about two hours. I'll call you back in a few to get the address. 'Bye."

He hung up the phone and looked down at her. Annie thought she read a mixture of worry mixed with fear in his eyes. "Looks like you're going to have to cancel your appointments this morning after all," he said quietly. "That was the private detective.

He just finished talking to Marcia's mother in Baton Rouge. She says Marcia just got there last night and told them the baby was with friends. The poor woman was in shock to learn otherwise, and she hopes we can bring the baby.''

"I guess we'd better get moving then," Annie said. All the lovely heat from West's lovemaking was wasted as she went cold inside. Over the past week, no matter how much she'd tried to avoid getting involved, she'd grown fond of Teddy, and giving him back was going to be difficult. But she had West now, and she would get through it.

She would get both of them through it.

"I'm surprised you aren't upset," West said, pushing off her. He settled back against the pillows as he watched her rise from the bed.

"I've been through this once before, West," she said, walking over to his closet where she'd hung the tailored suit she'd planned to wear to work. "I went into this knowing that Marcia loved Teddy, and she *would* want him back." Carrying the suit back to the bed, she hung it on the bedpost and stared at him. "Are you all right with this?"

"I'll tell you after I hear what Marcia says."

"Are you all right with *us?*" she asked, holding her breath, praying that he would admit that he might feel something strong for her. She wouldn't even ask for love—not yet anyway. But she wanted to know if they had a future.

West's deep blue eyes darkened to black. "I don't want you to leave me" was all he said. Annie wished she could feel comforted by those words, but she could tell as he rose from the bed and grabbed his clothes from the dresser drawer that he was still holding something back. She could only hope that what he hadn't said wasn't far more important that what he had.

"First, let me make it clear that I didn't let Marcia know that you were comin', Mr. Gallagher," Marcia's mother said, ushering them inside her modest three-bedroom home near Louisiana State University. "She said she had an errand and would be back in about a half hour, which is fine. I wanted the opportunity to get things straightened out with you first." She led the three of them into the small living room, and waved her hand toward the seats. West took an armchair across from the sofa, leaving it for Annie and the baby. Sitting next to her grandson, Mrs. Kinster tentatively, almost shyly, reached out and touched the back of Teddy's head.

"This is the first I've seen him in over three months," she said, smiling down at the boy. "I didn't even know Marcia was in town until last night when her hotel money ran out and she came here. She said she'd left the baby with friends, but she wouldn't tell me who. When the private detective called on your behalf, I was totally shocked." She glanced almost apologetically at Annie. "She didn't mention about her lawyer helpin' to care for Teddy."

"She probably didn't realize I would." Annie turned Teddy around so he could see his grandmother better, and Mrs. Kinster, a petite, nicely dressed brunette with Marcia's eyes, leaned forward and let

Teddy grip her finger. It was then Annie noticed that West was frowning at her. She sent him a return look that said no, it wasn't looking good for Marcia, and, client of hers or not, she knew it.

And Mrs. Kinster needed to know how bad things were, so Annie filled her in on how Teddy had come to be left with West.

Mrs. Kinster's mouth dropped open and her hand returned to her lap. She looked totally shocked. ''What on earth could possibly have gotten into her?'' she said in a soft voice, as though the breath had been knocked out of her.

Annie wanted to reassure her, but she couldn't. ''Basically, I'm afraid, Marcia abandoned her son, and if West and I hadn't made an agreement to keep Teddy out of the social welfare system until she returned, he would be in foster care now.''

Mrs. Kinster was pale as she put her hand to her mouth.

''Did she say why she left the baby at all?'' Annie asked. ''Or why she just didn't bring him here to you?''

She shook her head. ''Only that she was in town tryin' to do what she's desperately wanted to do for a long time, and that I was going to be very proud of her. I assumed she meant registerin' at the university.'' She sighed. ''Well, this just can't be. Even if she is goin' back to school, she's in big trouble now, and she's goin' to have to face it.'' She looked from West to Annie. ''Please accept my apologies on behalf of my daughter. She had no right to do what she did, and I'm goin' to make certain she understands that.''

While Teddy started babbling loudly, with emphasis, Mrs. Kinster nodded at him sadly. ''I know honey, I know. Your mama messed up.'' She looked from West to Annie. ''You're the lawyer—do you have any suggestions?''

''Would you agree to take custody of Teddy while Marcia gets some counseling?''

''I already told Marcia, plenty of times, that she could move back in here and work, and I would be happy to take care of Teddy. I've always believed in keepin' children as close to relatives as possible. But, no, she said she wanted to move to New Orleans. She said if she lived here, she would be too tempted to ask for my help all the time, and she wanted to grow up.'' Her eyes grew wistful. ''Apparently she just isn't ready.''

''Maybe she just got overwhelmed,'' Annie said, feeling a renewed stab of guilt that she hadn't helped her more. ''It doesn't excuse her leaving Teddy, but at least it explains it.''

''Well, she's got to understand she can't be doing that ever again. A child isn't something that can be tossed around and treated like a pile of laundry.''

''Amen,'' West said quietly.

Marcia's mother reached down and caressed Teddy again, and then seemed to consider something. ''If y'all will excuse me for just a minute, I'm headin' into the kitchen to call my husband, so we're both here when Marcia comes back.''

When they were alone, West leaned forward. "She seems sincere enough, Annie. What do you think?"

"I think we ought to see if Mr. Kinster is of the same mind as his wife. If he is, I'm willing to take a chance on leaving Teddy with them—as long as Marcia gets counseling on parental responsibilities."

He nodded slowly. Since Teddy was starting to squirm, Annie put him down on the carpet and let him crawl, staying near him so he didn't pull anything down on his head in the non-child-proofed room.

With all the bending Annie had to do, West was catching a view of every conceivable angle of her derriere in her slim-fitting business skirt as she chased after the baby, and his body was beginning to react. He cursed under his breath, because even though he wanted her more than ever, he knew he had some serious thinking to do about their situation. Trying to do the thinking now while watching her was next to impossible.

But if he didn't think about Annie, his mind mulled over losing Teddy, and that was just as bad. This week he had learned what it was like to love a baby— or at least the little charmer's cooing, his babbling, and the way he grinned at West when he picked him up. Then two days earlier than they'd expected, sure enough, West was losing that love in his life again, and the pain of it was smacking him hard, right in his heart. Oh, sure, he'd known they'd be giving Teddy back, but damn, he'd forgotten how painful the hurt could be.

Leaning back in his chair, he took a deep breath and tried not to think about anything.

Mrs. Kinster came back into the room with a tray of ice tea and glasses, and set it on the table. "I hope this is all right. With Teddy around, I'd just as soon not serve hot coffee."

"Ice tea is fine," Annie said, scooping Teddy up off the floor. "Would you like to hold him while we wait for Marcia and her father?"

"Of course," the woman said, reaching out. Whether she reminded Teddy of his mother, or he remembered his grandmother, or Teddy was just one sweet baby, Annie didn't know, but Teddy opened his arms and hugged Mrs. Kinster around her neck. Annie sighed deeply, and just barely kept her eyes from clouding up.

She glanced at West to see how he was holding up. Their eyes met across the room, and she saw the emptiness in his—like he didn't want to give Teddy up? The thought gave her new hope. If he had actually enjoyed having the baby in his life, maybe he would take a chance on his own future....

The front door opened suddenly and Marcia's voice filtered through the rooms, filled with excitement. "Mama, where are you? I've got wonderful news."

"The livin' room," Mrs. Kinster called.

"I've done it, Mama—I'm getting married! I've made my own dream come true—" Marcia's voice dropped off as she reached the doorway and stopped dead in her tracks. "Oh, my Lord," she said in a reverent voice. "I guess I also created my own little nightmare, didn't I?"

The house was in chaos for a while as Marcia kissed and hugged Teddy and then Marcia's father arrived and had to be filled in by Mrs. Kinster. But finally the whole group gathered in the living room to hear Marcia's story of what she'd been doing for the past week.

Giving one last smile to her fiancé, Jord Ames, a young man who had come in a few minutes after her and sat down next to her, Marcia finally started.

"Well, this all began a few months ago when I heard that Jord here was comin' back to Baton Rouge for only two weeks. I wanted to go see him to tell him that I'd gotten pregnant and had his baby, but he'd always said he didn't want kids until he could afford them. So I was scared he'd be mad that I hadn't given Teddy up for adoption—as if I could ever do that." She stopped to give her son a warm smile. "But then I took Mr. Gallagher's seminar about goin' after your dream, and I knew I couldn't let Teddy grow up without a daddy. It would be just too sad for my baby and me. So I planned it out and really concentrated on what I wanted most, and I figured out I had to get Jord to marry me before he went back overseas in the army so Teddy would have his daddy."

West took another look at the young couple. Jord Ames was feeding Teddy, staring at his son as though he were in awe, and something inside West suddenly began to ache. *Marcia had gone through all this just for Teddy.* A baby now had a daddy because of *his* seminar. What he was doing was helping people. He'd done Joseph Hayden, his teacher back in high school, proud.

But that fact gave West little satisfaction. He had to wonder if a marriage between these two would last. He'd grabbed an opportunity to speak to Jord earlier, and found out that Marcia had taken great care to keep Teddy's existence a total secret from him and everyone they knew by going upstate to her grandmother's to have Teddy and then moving to New Orleans shortly after. Jord had been horrified that his new fiancée had left his son anywhere, even with what she considered the best intentions. West knew that any relationship took a great deal of maturity, and even though Jord might be okay in that department, his young, soon-to-be wife had a great deal of growing up to do. If Jord got sick of waiting for Marcia to get her act together, Teddy might end up without a daddy again.

The thought made him sick.

"But what possessed you to leave your baby behind with Mr. Gallagher?" Marcia's father asked. West could feel the man's frustration vibrating over to his daughter, who for the first time seemed to sense the seriousness of what she'd done. "And don't give me any song and dance about how nice Mr. Gallagher was again," he added. "You knew better than to leave a helpless infant on anyone's doorstep."

"I couldn't bring Teddy here, Daddy," Marcia said slowly. "I had to get Jord to want to marry me myself, and I couldn't have you or Mama helpin' it along or takin' matters into your own hands by lurin' him over to see his son." She looked at each of her parents. "I really blew it, I know. It wasn't the best thing to do."

"Not the best thing to do?" Marcia's father shook his head, his voice grave with distress. "What if someone had seen my little grandson out there and toted him—"

"Excuse me, sir," Jord interrupted. When Mr. Kinster fluttered his hands as if to say "Go ahead"—or more like, West thought, "I give up"—Jord turned to his fiancée. "Marcia, you should have come to me when you first got pregnant. I told you from the start that I loved you and was enlisting so we would have a steady income, and in a year or two, when I was sure I was set, I wanted to get married. That's why I came back to Baton Rouge—to get you."

Her mouth twisting in anguish, tears rolling over the blush on her cheeks, Marcia looked around. "I am sorry."

"In the future, Marcia," Jord said quietly, "come to me. When we get married, it will be because I want to, not because of the baby." Breaking his gaze, he looked proudly down at his son, and his lips turned up at the edges. "Although he's a great bonus."

"So we all live happily ever after?" Marcia said hopefully.

"Not quite," Mrs. Kinster said. "You were lucky this time, Marcia. But there can't be a next. Had Mr. Gallagher and Ms. Robicheaux had a mind to, they could have turned Teddy over to the social welfare system as an abandoned child, and Teddy would be in foster care right now."

"Oh, my Lord," Marcia said, her face reddening. "I never meant to abandon him! I wouldn't have left him with just anyone. Mr. Gallagher is famous! I knew he'd take great care of Teddy.''

The price of fame, West thought with an inward groan. Seeing his face, Annie gave him a short, sympathetic smile.

''Be that as it may, Ms. Robicheaux has suggested counseling and us taking care of the baby until you're finished. Your father has already agreed.''

''But Jord has to go back overseas in three days!''

Jord was the first one to shake his head. ''I think you'd best do what they say, Marcia. You couldn't have come with me right away anyway—I told you it takes a while to secure housing and all for the three of us. How about if you follow Ms. Robicheaux's suggestions here and when they think it's okay, I'll come back and we'll get married then.''

Marcia wasn't thrilled, but she knew Jord was only asking out of politeness. She didn't have a choice, she could see it in the face of everyone around her. She would have to do something to prove to her parents and Jord that she was a good, caring mother. So she agreed.

That meant that Annie and West finally felt free to leave Teddy with his grandparents. But before they did, as they'd discussed on the way over, West and Annie excused themselves, went out to his car, and brought in the playpen, car seat, and Teddy's clothes for the young parents. Annie explained where they'd come from.

''Oh, my gosh, I got so excited when I left, I never even thought about his needin' all that stuff,'' Marcia said thickly. She sat down with a grim look on her face. "But they're brand new," she added. "Maybe you could just sell them and get some of your money back." Her face lit up. "Or maybe you can keep them up in your attic for when you have your first baby!"

Annie's heart slammed against her ribs. Blinking, unable to speak, she waited for West to say something, but wasn't sure he would, either. He'd been awfully quiet outside.

"Keep them," West said, his voice thick. "Consider it an engagement present from Annie and me."

"Thank you," Jord and Marcia said together, and then, spontaneously, Marcia came over and put a sleepy Teddy in Annie's arms.

Annie hugged the baby to her. With all his baby softness cradled against her breasts and the scent of baby powder drifting up toward her, she had to make a determined effort not to cry. Since she had no nieces or nephews, and, being with West, would have no children of her own, Teddy was likely to be the last baby she would grow close to. It hurt to know that.

But not having West, she knew, would hurt a lot more. So she kissed Teddy's cheek and handed him back to his mother with a soft goodbye, a goodbye that was meant for more than just Teddy. It was a goodbye to her dream of having a child.

The throaty, reverent way that Annie said farewell to Teddy tugged at West's heart as they left the Kinsters' and walked out to his car together. Just like him, Annie was hurting badly, but her pain wasn't just from giving up Teddy, West knew. It was also from a final surrendering of her dream of having a baby, and from making a commitment to him.

When Annie had first said she wanted him more than anything else, he'd felt like he'd won the lottery, had a birthday, and had woken up to find that his abandonment as a child had been nothing more than a nightmare, all at once. She'd filled the house he'd always wanted with love and warmth. She'd made the dream he'd had of having his own home once again come true.

But as wonderful as the past week had been for him, it had also been frightening. He'd had a real home, a family, and plenty of love once before. Then, suddenly, he'd been eight years old and alone, and it had taken him years to learn to manage the resulting anger and pain, pain that had always seemed to be circled around his neck and just short of squeezing the life out of him. Losing Teddy had brought it all back in a rush of overwhelming feeling. Losing Teddy had put the rope back around his neck.

He'd known better than to let himself care. He'd been fully aware that the noose of pain was forever dangling right above his head—never much farther away than that—which was why he'd vowed never to love anyone again in the first place. Keeping the pain at bay had meant keeping his life unencumbered. Since the day he'd gone into the first foster home alone, it had become his number one rule—don't get attached, because you'll only end up hurting. And never, ever love anything, because you'll lose it.

He'd gotten through years like that, damn it, West thought as he silently drove the interstate back to New Orleans, reaching out to people but never letting them touch him. But then had come Teddy, whose loss, he

was certain, had given him just a hint of what he'd
be in for if he let Annie totally into his life and then
he lost her—a blinding, choking, all-encompassing
kind of pain that was sure to bring him to his knees
and then shatter him. And this time, he didn't think
he could pull the pieces back together again.

Annie's pain from losing her heart's desire already
hung between them like a heavy mist of tears. No
matter what she claimed she wanted, if she never became a mother, West was sure the hurt would grow
and explode inside her, and what would blow up
would be their relationship. It was all so clear, and
West knew what he had to do to make sure Annie
would get the dream she so wanted, and so deserved.

He had to make certain she left him.

By the next morning, Annie came to the horrible
awareness that West was withdrawing from her. On
the way home from the Kinsters', and later, after
she'd gone to work and finally returned to West's,
she'd tried to talk to him about how he felt, but he
told her he didn't feel anything about giving up the
child—why should he? Teddy wasn't his.

But Annie had seen agony in his eyes, and known
better. The way he'd put up a wall around him so she
couldn't get close hurt, but she tried to understand.
He wasn't used to having love in his life. So last night
she'd cuddled up against him to reassure him that she,
at least, wasn't going to leave. He'd held her, but
made no move to touch her—not even a caress on
her cheek. When he was asleep, she cried silently,

alone, because she'd felt their relationship ebbing away.

And now, waiting for West to come down to breakfast, Annie was feeling the way she did before going into the courtroom to defend a client she knew was in big trouble. Her insides were clenched with tension, and her lips were so tightly pressed together they felt glued. She was worried. Apprehensive.

Oh, hell, she was just plain scared to death.

"What's wrong, West?" she asked softly when he came into the kitchen and she saw the guarded look covering the rugged angles of his face. This wasn't the West she knew. This was someone who was as scared as she felt now—and a hell of a lot more distant. "And please don't tell me there's nothing wrong, because there is, and we both know it."

West poured a cup of coffee, carried it to the table, and sat across from her. He didn't want to put either of them through this, but he knew he had to. For her sake. "I'm worried, Annie, that we aren't going to last, because you aren't going to accept that I don't want kids."

"Are you saying you don't want me?"

"I didn't say that," West said, pulling out each word. "I'm just trying to make sure it's straight between us about any future kids. I know you're hoping for the best from me, and I'm trying to tell you now, that the best is not in me to give."

Annie wanted to scream. While they'd had Teddy, West had started to open up his heart, she knew he had. He'd come so close to believing in love again. But now he was much like he'd been the night she'd met him—closed off, guarded. Giving up that baby must have reminded him of the pain of loss. The pain life could inflict.

She knew it well. She felt it now.

"Giving Teddy back hurt, I know, West. It hurt me, too."

"I know," he said, his voice quiet and faraway. "I watched you when you said goodbye to Teddy. I saw your face. Can you honestly tell me you'll be happy for the rest of your life never having a child?" His eyes searched hers as he waited for an answer.

"I'll give up having a child if it means I have your love."

He shook his head. "And you'll find that my love isn't enough. I saw your eyes, Annie. I read what was in your heart."

When she said goodbye to Teddy, he meant.

Rising, West walked to the window to gaze out and drink his coffee, his back to her. Wanting to convince him he was wrong, Annie got to her feet, crossed the floor, and put her hand on his shoulder, but West stiffened, showing no sign he wanted her to break down the wall he'd put up.

Annie dropped her hand. Given his background, she understood why he was withdrawing—he was scared he would give his heart to her and she would trample it running from him when she grew desperate to have a baby and he refused. It was all so crystal clear, and it made her ache to the bottom of her heart, for both him and her. Because her having a child in the future was not the real problem.

No, the real problem was that he couldn't trust her

to really love him, unconditionally. He was so determined that he wasn't going to be hurt again, he was locking up his heart and hiding the key. She didn't know how to reach him.

"You're lucky I know how to keep a stiff upper lip, West, otherwise you'd be dealing with some tears right now."

West said nothing, just continued to look out the window. But the fingers gripping the handle of his coffee mug were turning white.

"Maybe I will break down and cry," Annie said, biting her bottom lip. "It would serve you right. Maybe you'd finally be forced to deal with your emotions and take a chance, instead of retreating. Maybe tears would show you how much you mean to me."

He finally gazed down at her. "Annie, I'm sorry, but I can't change the way I am."

"The crime of that is, I think you'd like to. I think deep down you really want what your true dream is."

"And that is?"

"Just like what you wrote, your real dream *is* sometimes just what you're most afraid of. With you, West, that's not our having a child. What you're really afraid of is falling in love and being abandoned again. Not one thing I say or do is going to change that. Only you can."

West swore under his breath. "I know how I want my life to be, Annie, and I know about dreams."

"I don't think you do," she said, shaking her head sadly. "Either that, or you've forgotten the best part of your book. But unless you go back, reread it, and figure out how to help yourself, I can't let our relationship continue. I don't want to stay with a man who won't trust in the power of love. Thinking I'm going to hurt you, you'll always be suspicious of me, ready to withdraw.'' The tears finally did come then, spilling over, and Annie wiped them away impatiently. ''I'm leaving.''

Hating himself for making Annie cry, West watched her go into the living room. It was over. As much as he wanted to think this was for the best, all he could feel was the unrelenting, agonizing pain…all too familiar…the pain he'd been expecting all night.

Only this time he had only himself to blame.

Slamming his fist down, he heard rather than felt the coffee mug shatter against the steel sink. As he stared down at the scattered pieces of brown ceramic, West cursed the day he was born.

10

—◆—

Gigi swept into Annie's office minus her accent and sporting another look-at-me dress, a wide-skirted, lemon chiffon that actually looked beautiful with her masses of auburn hair. "Darling, I need to talk to you."

"You didn't have to dress up for that, Aunt Gigi," Annie said, giving her a forced smile—she couldn't conjure up the real thing after almost two point five days of being without West—and bending back over the list she'd been looking at. "I keep things pretty casual here on Sundays," she added as she scratched out an item she'd finished and added another "to do" for tomorrow. "Of course, even I occasionally have to dress up for court, but even so, lemon chiffon might be overdoing it—"

"West Gallagher called me."

Annie's widened eyes flew up to stare at Gigi. She'd spent two long days that had stretched into even longer evenings at work, because her apartment felt too empty to go home to. Racking her brain, trying to find some way to convince West they were meant for each other, had turned her into an insomniac. Her nerves were stretched thin, and she was in no mood for a joke—not even one of her aunt's.

"Don't try to wreck my good mood with teasing, Aunt Gigi," she said dryly. "If I get any happier, you may have to bury me."

"Yes, I can see how happy you are. This is New Orleans, you know. People are superstitious. Better start putting some cover stick on those shadows under your eyes, honey, or your clients are going to think you're one of the walking dead."

"I am."

"He did call, Annie." Gigi's eyes possessed not even a hint of the twinkle that Annie previously thought had taken up permanent residence there. Her aunt was not lying to her.

"What did he want?" Annie asked, barely recognizing her voice. "Has he come to his senses yet?"

"He asked me if I knew anything about a part of his book you quoted that he never wrote. The part about your real dream being what you're most afraid of having."

"He didn't write that?"

Gigi shook her head slowly, precisely, and the coral lips of her mouth twisted in a smile. "Believe it or not, I came up with that myself, just for you. I wanted you to examine what you were going after—this baby wish of yours. But you always think everyone knows more than I do, so I told you West wrote it because I figured you'd listen to him."

"Oh, Aunt Gigi." Sitting back in her chair, Annie burst into soft laughter. "Poor West. I told him he wrote it and that he should follow his own advice. If he finally resorted to calling you, he must have been going crazy trying to find it in his book.''

''More like he's been going crazy missing you.''

''Did he say that?''

Gigi waved her hand in the air. ''Men. Do they ever say what they mean?''

''West does. West is a great talker.'' Annie took a deep breath and sighed. Good Lord, she missed him. ''That's all he wanted?''

''It's enough. If he's obsessing about what you told him enough to call me, honey, he's thinking about you.'' Reaching across Annie's desk, Gigi patted her hand. ''It'll work out.''

''How do you know?''

''Think of your life so far, Annie. You put up with Jean-Pierre's laziness long after you should have left because his daughter needed you. You became a lawyer so you could help people who need you. And you wanted a baby so someone would need you. Everything you've ever done in life has been connected with wanting to be loved and needed. Am I right?''

Annie nodded slowly. Gigi had to be. She certainly couldn't think of any other explanations for the choices she'd made in her life. Every one of them seemed to stem from the fact that her parents hadn't wanted her or needed her, and somehow, someway, she was going to find people who did.

''That's why I think it's going to work out,'' Gigi said. ''You figured out having a baby *wasn't* your real dream—falling in love was. You were just wary of getting involved with another man who really didn't need or want you. But West does, doesn't he?''

"I think so," Annie said, nodding.

"Of course he does. West wants love more than anything else, and he knows he can have that with you, he's just frightened. The key to getting him back is to eliminate his fear about it. Then you two will be free to be happy."

Considering that, Annie leaned against the padded back of her chair, while Gigi glanced down at her dainty watch and moaned. "Look at the time—I've got to get to my performance." Her black patent leather purse in hand, she stood. "Call me and let me know if you figure anything out."

Rising, Annie followed her to the door. "I love you, Aunt Gigi."

"I love you, too, honey." Gigi stopped long enough to push a tendril of Annie's hair behind her ear. "Stop worrying—you'll think of something. You have to—you and West are destined to be together. I read West's bio in his book. You both started with similar backgrounds, and you've both become successes, and he can understand you and your life better than any other man can. If ever two people deserve each other's love, it's you and West. He's just scared right now. Don't give up."

"I won't," Annie whispered.

Gigi wiggled her fingers and turned to go.

"Aunt Gigi?"

Gigi swirled around, her skirt billowing like a lemon cloud around her.

"West and I may have started the same way, only I was lucky enough to get another mother—you. West didn't have anyone."

"He does now, honey." Gigi's face went bright-eyed with pride. "He has you."

Blinking back yet another set of tears, Annie smiled at her aunt and waited until she was on the elevator before locking the door to her office. Sitting down behind her desk, she picked up a pen and started to write again, but the only thing on her mind was what her aunt had suggested she do to win West back.

She'd already tried becoming the dream West wanted—she'd loved him with all her might. But eliminating the fear that accompanied her loving him—that had her stumped. She thought it meant she had to convince him she would stick with him through the best and the worst. But how could she do that? How on earth?

A seed of an idea sprouted and took root as Annie considered it. What she wanted to do might only make West mad, not totally convince him they had a future together. On the other hand, it would prove her point, and it would be a great deal of trouble for him to undo.

It might be easier for him to let her stay.

Of course, she would need her aunt's help and Gigi had been headed toward a busy evening. But that was all right. Tonight she would plan, and tomorrow she would contact Aunt Gigi and take her last shot at happiness.

West paced up and down his rug and finally tossed his notes on the couch in disgust. He might as well hang up his career; he'd lost the ability to concentrate.

When he'd broken down and called Gigi the day before, he'd told himself it was because he had to know where Annie'd gotten that idea about a person's real dream, but he could no longer kid himself. He had been two seconds from asking Gigi if Annie was as miserable as he.

Of course, he'd said goodbye and hung up before he'd made that mistake, but then he'd spent the rest of the day thinking about Gigi's theory.

What was it he wanted but feared most?

To have a home no one could ever take him out of had been his dream. But judging by the way he was feeling now, all dead inside, without Annie in it, his home had become his tomb. It had probably always been that way, but before Annie—and hell, yes, before Teddy—he hadn't known enough to realize the difference.

But back to his real dream. What did he really want, but was scared to death to have? Was Annie right? Was it love?

It was love, he realized with a sinking feeling. Annie's love. He wasn't hungry, he couldn't concentrate, and he didn't even care if he ever gave another seminar. Motivating people to go after their dreams seemed worthless, since he wasn't destined to have his. He started to shake, because to make his dream come true, he was going to have to risk putting all his feelings on the line, totally commit his heart to Annie, and never worry about her abandoning him again. Until he did, he'd never get her back. But could he do what she said? Could he let go and trust in love again?

The doorbell rang. Frowning, he considered not answering it, half expecting a repeat of last Friday night, when the delivery of a child had turned his world upside down. But the bell pealed again, over and over, and then a fist pounded against the wood. Someone really wanted him to answer. Striding to the door, exasperated, he swung it open.

"Matt!" His brother. The last person he'd expected to see on his doorstep—but maybe he needed a diversion. Maybe, in fact, Matt could help. "C'mon in," he added, stepping aside.

"Gina's with me." Matthew, a lean and slightly shorter version of West, stepped inside, followed by his wife, a petite, dark-haired woman with a great smile. "I know you said the timing wasn't right to come, but Gina said it was, and I'm sorry. You might be my brother, but I'm married to her. She outvotes you."

"Hello, West." Gina was shining that great smile his way, so West smiled back, but his attention was really on his brother. He was supposed to be the outgoing sibling, the one who was good with people, but he didn't know how to handle this moment. It was only the second time he'd seen Matt in the past twenty years, and the other time had been at Matt's wedding, when they hadn't had much time together. They were relative strangers.

"Oh, good Lord, you two," Gina said, her voice as bright as her smile. "You're family and this is the nineties. You can hug each other, even if this isn't a special occasion."

West did.

"Now me." Gina reached up and hugged him. While she'd always been sweetly curvy, West sensed there was a whole lot more of her than a few months ago when he'd hugged her at the wedding. Frowning, he pulled back and looked at his sister-in-law. There was a soft glow in her cheeks and a roundness of her stomach under her oversize T-shirt.

He swallowed down a suddenly dry throat.

"Surprise, West," Gina said, not having to specify what the surprise was. He was going to be an uncle.

A bunch of emotions rocketed through West as he stared first at Matthew, and then back at Gina. Stunned, he was both excited and worried for his brother all at once. Then the worry won out and choked him up so that he couldn't speak.

Gina tugged on West's sleeve. "The next things you're supposed to say are, 'That's wonderful you two, congratulations, and I'd love to pay for his college tuition.'"

He gazed down at her. "If you ever need money for the baby, of course I'll help you, Gina."

"I was teasing!" Gina protested in horror. Her huge dark eyes flew to her husband. "Matt, tell him I was just joking!"

"Well, if he's offering us money…" Matt said with a look of inevitability at his wife, "who am I to protest? He purportedly made a fortune on that book of his, so why should we struggle?"

"*Now* you develop a sense of humor." But she quickly forgot her husband in lieu of West, who had won her full attention with his silence. "Are you really upset with us for coming?" she asked.

''No, no, not at all,'' West denied. He *was* worried though—about their baby and about the future of his brother's marriage. Matthew and Gina currently had a commuter marriage, with Matt, an air-force pilot, flying all the time out of Virginia, and Gina running her bridal shop in Ohio. He had to ask. ''With the baby coming, you aren't going to keep things as they've been, are you?''

''That's the other reason we came to New Orleans, West,'' Matt said, slipping his arm around Gina and pulling her close. ''I'm interviewing for a job flying for a commuter airline. If I take it, Gina plans to sell her house and her business to her manager, and we'll be neighbors. She wants to be a full-time mother.''

Full-time mother. Thinking about Annie and her dream that would never be, West's misery doubled up its fist and punched him in the gut. ''You're moving here because of me?'' he asked, his throat tight, torn between agony about Annie and happiness over having his brother near again.

''That's right,'' Gina said. ''You once said you're staying put now, and twenty years is way too long for two brothers to be separated.'' Reaching up, she patted him on the cheek. ''Be nice about this, or we'll move in next door and spy on all your dates.''

Leaning down, West gave her a quick kiss on the cheek. ''Is that nice enough?''

She sighed, delighted. ''You Gallagher boys can be such charmers when you want to be. So you really don't mind that we came?''

''No, I really don't mind.'' He managed a smile, because he knew the two of them expected it, but his heart was somewhere else and his mind was on the emptiness that stretched before him in his own life.

"You really look peaked," Gina said to West. "Maybe you ought to sit down. Can I get you something to drink?"

"I should be saying that to you, shouldn't I?" he asked. His manners had been shot to hell along with his spirit. "Look, let me get *you* something—"

Gina was shaking her head. "I'll find my way to the kitchen and get my own. That will give you and Matt a chance to talk." She dropped her purse near the wall. With another smile that came from being completely happy with her life directed at her husband, she blew him a kiss and headed off in the direction West pointed.

"Gina might not want to sit down, but I think I want to," Matt said, stretching. "I swear that woman has more energy than a jet engine."

West, his mind busy sorting out everything he'd just heard, walked into his living room and plopped down in his favorite armchair. He was glad he'd be seeing Matt on a regular basis, and that Matt and Gina were setting up a great life for their child-to-be. He just wished he could understand how his brother had reconciled their past to the point where it didn't bother him to have a child.

Apparently not as tired as he thought, Matt walked over to survey West's model car collection. "Nice. I make model planes myself."

West looked up at the man he barely knew. Oh, sure, Matt had filled him in on the peripheral stuff— how his brother had ended up on the streets after being labeled bad, and how he'd gone from there to marrying Gina, but only after they almost hadn't made it. All that West knew.

But he and Matt had been strangers for twenty years, and the man Matt had become, West did not know—except for a couple important things. His loyal brother had never forgotten him, and had never stopped looking for him, and West was very glad to have his brother close again.

"So, while Gina's busy," Matt said, plopping down on the sofa across from West, "tell me what's really going on."

As his brother's keen blue eyes surveyed him, waiting patiently, West struggled to figure out where to begin.

"I'm miserable."

A semblance of a smile shadowed his brother's lips. "Yeah, I can tell. You look like you used to when you thought I was going to get us in big trouble. Halfway between wanting to cry and wanting to beat somebody up."

"I was only eight," West said in defense, half grinning. But just as swiftly, he sobered. "I've gotten myself in big trouble."

Matt sat back and crossed one ankle over his knee. "Let me guess. Since you've turned into a fine, upstanding citizen whom people trust with little babies, this can't be legal trouble. You've already told me you wouldn't touch booze with a ten-foot pole after what our father put us through. Gee, what's left?" He snapped his fingers. "A woman, right? No, wait, let me narrow that down—the same Annie who's 'just a friend'?"

"Yeah." West gave him an abbreviated version of what had really been going on during the past week.

"So you're miserable without her." Matt stood and started pacing. "But you're afraid to marry her, because you think she'll grow to hate you and then leave you if you don't have children. But you don't want kids." He paused and switched direction. "Because you don't want a repeat of what happened to us if you two split up. On the other hand..." He paused again and walked toward West, where he stopped. "You'd be perfectly willing to live with her, if you thought she really didn't want kids. You're afraid to take a chance either way."

"That about sums it up." West nodded.

"From the looks of it, offhand I'd say you're in love." Matt gave him a long look. "Either that, or you're real confused."

For the first time since Annie had left, West chuckled. "Hell, I figured both of those out without your help. You have any other suggestions?"

Matt shook his head. "Besides talking to Gina, who's the smartest woman I know when it comes to stuff like this, I'm afraid I don't."

"But you're not afraid of splitting with Gina and having your kid go through the agony of a broken family. Why not?"

"Because I keep in mind we aren't our parents," Matt said simply. "I learned not to run from what I want and need, and Gina has always been self-sufficient. No child of ours will ever have to suffer like we did.''

That was true, West thought, rising to pace the room himself as Matthew sat down.

Matt raised his eyes in sudden concern. ''You have forgiven our parents, haven't you?''

West shrugged his broad shoulders. ''I was glad when I heard Gina helped them reconcile, but I don't think we'll ever be that close. I did send Mom a Mother's Day card and some flowers. I want them to be happy. So, yeah, I guess I've forgiven them.''

''Then you realize that you and Annie aren't them, either, and you'll handle things differently in your marriage.''

''I know that. On the other hand—''

''On the other hand, nothing,'' Matt said forcefully. ''You're making this too complicated. You say you don't want to put any child of yours through the kind of hurt you went through, but you never will. You aren't that kind of man. Is Annie that kind of woman?''

''No.''

''Then you should trust her.''

His back to his brother, West swallowed, stopped, and stared blankly at his classic car collection. He had to know.

''How did you do it, Matt?'' he asked, turning to watch his brother's reaction. ''How did you come out of the past we had, able to go happily into a normal future, when I can't get my act together?''

''Simple.'' Matt rose as Gina joined them, carrying two glasses of ice tea. When she set them down, he slipped his arm around her waist and pulled her close. "Love."

The sudden knock on the front door caught them all by surprise, and West swore. Apparently no one was going to let him bask in misery alone today.

He pulled it open. "Gigi!"

"It ees awful," she said, annihilating the second last word. "My Annee says she needs you to come, but she could not find your unlisted phone number, and it has something to do with that poor little *babee!*" Gigi swept through his door and into his living room, stopping when she saw Matt and Gina.

"Hello."

"Hello," Matt said. "Are you a friend of Annie's?"

"I'm her aunt Gigi. You have met her?"

"No, not yet, but I must admit, I'm becoming really eager to. Is she French, too?" Matt turned to his wife. "You didn't tell me Annie sounded French on the phone."

"She didn't." Gina shook her head.

"That's because she isn't French!" West said, feeling like he was back in the Twilight Zone. "Neither is Gigi."

"Gigi sounds French," Matt observed. "Doesn't she, Gina?"

"She certainly does," Gina said, giving him her sweetest smile and taking a sip of her ice tea.

Aunt Gigi beamed at the two of them. "And you two are?"

"Matt is my brother," West said, "and Gina is his wife." Sighing, West put his hands on Gigi's shoulders, hoping to focus her back on the matter at hand, even though he highly suspected most of Gigi's persona was a huge act and she was smarter than the rest of them combined.

"I'm assuming by 'poor little babee,'" he said to Gigi, "you mean Teddy. And as far as Annee—" He stopped and corrected himself, sounding exasperated. "*Annie*—is she all right?"

"Oh, *oui*, Annie. She called from—" Gigi reached into her purse and pulled out a slip of paper. "From this shopping center on this street and said that she needs you to come. Please, please go, even if you are annoyed with Marcia for leaving poor babee Teddy on your doorstep."

"Someone left a baby on your doorstep?" Gina asked, her mouth falling open in shock as she put both hands protectively over her stomach. "How could anyone?"

"I'll explain later," Matt said, grinning. "This place is better than an amusement park."

"I'd better go find out what's up," West said. He needed some air anyway. "Are you coming, Gigi?"

"Please, no, she said she wanted you, not me. I will wait here in case you miss each other and she comes here."

West wasn't sure that made sense, but he didn't want to take the time to figure out Aunt Gigi—assuming that was possible.

"Matt?"

"Sure, I'll go—" Matt oomphed overdramatically as Gina lightly elbowed him.

"No," Gina said. "The two of us need to rest for

a while. But you can take our car. It's blocking yours.''

Matt tossed West the keys, and West headed outside, leaving the door open. Gigi left the room to shut it.

Grinning at his wife, Matt said, ''I have to admit, Gina, I'm almost feeling sorry for West. I don't think even I had to go through this much for love.''

''What about when the whole neighborhood was watching us in the treehouse?'' Gina asked, watching Annie's aunt as she rejoined them.

''Peanuts compared to this,'' Matt said, giving her a quick kiss. ''But worth every minute. Now tell me why you didn't want me to go with West.''

''Because it's a chance for West and Annie to be alone—if she really is there.''

''Huh?'' Matt asked. But Gina's keen eyes watched Gigi, who merely smiled and didn't comment.

''Just as I thought!'' Gina said triumphantly. ''West may be so lovestruck he isn't thinking straight, and Matt's a man, so he would never suspect a setup here—''

''Hey, I resent that,'' he said, ruffling his fingers through Gina's short, dark brown hair.

Gina shot him a fond smile and turned to Gigi. ''But you can't fool me. What's really going on? And please tell me it's nothing we're going to have to stand up for, because really, my feet are starting to kill me.''

Aunt Gigi's mouth curved into a smile. She'd been taken aback at their presence when she'd arrived, but now—well, since they so obviously cared about

West's happiness, Gigi thought they might come in handy.

"I'll explain everything," Gigi told them. "Only I have to hurry, because we don't have a whole lot of time."

"Her accent's gone," Matt whispered.

"Oh, I only do that around West," Gigi said, sitting next to Gina. "He expects it as part of eccentric Aunt Gigi."

Gina and Matt grinned and sat back to listen.

Well over an hour later, just after dark fell, West turned onto his street, vacillating between feeling furious at Gigi, confused as hell, and depressed. There had been no sign of Teddy or Annie, and he couldn't figure out why on earth Gigi would send him on a wild-goose chase. He supposed Annie might really have sent for him and then needed to leave before he got there, but hell, it was hard to believe.

While he'd been waiting and looking for her, he'd thought about nothing but a future that looked pretty bleak to him, and about what his brother had said. He wanted to go to Annie, tell her he was ready to try with her, but he thought she might turn him away just like he'd driven her out of his life. He wouldn't blame her one bit.

Parking Matt's car in the driveway, West got out, shut the door and rounded the hood to head up the walk to the front entrance. He was halfway there when he looked up at his porch...and stopped where he was, his every limb freezing when he saw it.

Another large-size wicker basket. Another blanket

over the top. Another note attached by tape to the handle, flapping in the breeze.

Oh, no, West thought, everything inside him telling him to run away. He didn't deserve this. He'd stopped writing checks with his name and address on them at the market. He hadn't even done his infomercial yet. This couldn't be happening again.

He took a few tentative steps forward. The blanket moved, and he groaned inwardly. Why him? This time, he *was* whining, and he no longer cared. But this time, he thought he knew the answer to the question.

Why him? Because he was being cursed for not accepting love into his life when he'd had a chance. This was fate's way of getting even, teaching him to accept love in his life by making him relive the same lesson over and over again.

"Okay," he said loudly to whoever it was who was in control of his life, because it sure wasn't him anymore. "I'm giving up here. I want Annie Robicheaux back in my life for as long as she can stand me—just please, whoever left this basket, come and take it back!"

"Too late." Annie's soft voice came from amid the tall shrubbery. She stepped out into the warm, glowing circle of the porch light where he could see her.

Their eyes met, and he lost his fear. "You weren't waiting for me at the supermarket, and there was never any problem, was there, Annie?"

"Oh, but there was," Annie corrected, nodding her head. "Maybe not the kind Gigi told you, but yes, if you and I were going to remain apart, I would say there was a *big* problem. But I heard what you said just now, and I think maybe we've both found our solutions. Go ahead, read the note.''

Held by the hazel warmth of her eyes, he leaned over and grabbed the note, holding it up to where he could read it. Only then did he break eye contact.

Dear West,
Aunt Gigi suggested I find the biggest fear you have about the dream you want and eliminate it, and then maybe we would be free to be happy together. We both know we want each other, but you were afraid I would leave you—and then, last Saturday, I made a big mistake by doing exactly that.

But I'm back to fix it. I hope you adore the baby in this basket, and me, because you're stuck with the both of us. We will both remain loyal to the end, I promise. And don't worry. If you'll only trust in the power of love, there's nothing in this basket the two of us can't handle together.

I love you.

Annie had signed it. Taking a deep breath, West leaned over and pulled the blanket off the basket. There, on top of a heap of old cushions, was a puppy, a small, golden cocker spaniel, curled up and sleeping peacefully.

Straightening, a whisper of a smile curving his mouth, West folded the note into fourths and stuck it in the inside pocket of his blazer, next to his heart.

Then he opened his arms to Annie, who half ran into them, and sighed as he pulled her close.

"He's perfect, Annie," he uttered throatily. "And so are you."

"It's going to be all right, West," she said softly, with all her heart. "I promise."

"I might not have known that before, but I know it now."

She pulled back and gave him a questioning look.

"I know it will, because when Gigi told me you needed me, I rushed to help you like you were tied to train tracks and the express was coming through. I know, because when you weren't at the supermarket, I wanted to go to you, but then I thought about how I'd driven you out and thought I'd lost you forever." He smiled. "And if that isn't enough, I know... because I love you, and I want to make your other dream come true—for both of us."

"A baby?" she asked, her voice trembling.

"A baby," he confirmed. "Besides, dogs need children around them, don't they?"

Laughing, she curled her arms around his neck and kissed him, a kiss to seal their love, a kiss that made West realize that whatever had happened to him before, and whatever was to come, Annie would be his, forever.

They were kissing again when they heard a thump at the window. Breaking the kiss, West kept his arms around Annie. "That was Aunt Gigi. I guess we should go inside and let them know what's going on," he suggested reluctantly.

"I think they can wait," Annie said, pulling him

closer. "Besides, I have something to warn you about before you go in."

"Am I going to like it?"

"I don't know," she said, finding it awfully hard to think with his lips dotting kisses near her ear. She pulled back from him just a little. "Your sister-in-law and Aunt Gigi sure thought what I did was great—but then, it was Gigi's idea. That's why she got you out of the house, so I would have time to pull it off. Now your brother, on the other hand, just sort of stood around looking outnumbered."

The unflappable Matt? His fighter-pilot brother? "This must be really interesting if it fazed him. I like it already."

"Good. Because either you'll have to accept it, or you'll have to formally evict me and throw my furniture out on your front lawn. I'm not leaving you again."

"You moved in?"

"Lock, stock, and a negligee picked out by Aunt Gigi." She smiled when his eyes lit up. "A little housewarming present."

"Another dream come true." He pulled her against him for another long kiss. "And as for evicting you…"

She nodded.

"Who am I to fight the system?"

Epilogue

◀━━▶

"Christmas card catch-up, and then I'll give you your present," Annie announced to West, who was holding their eight-month-old son Zach and dodging his curious fingers, which were exploring West's ear. They were at the kitchen table, waiting for Gina and Matt to change their own son, two-year-old Wyatt, into dress clothes so they could take family Christmas Eve pictures.

"Am I going to like this present?"

"I think so. Aunt Gigi had nothing to do with this one, I promise you."

"That's too bad," West said, meaning it. Even though she was very busy singing and being happily married to Nigel, the maître d' who had chased West through the Café Lauree that long-ago night, Gigi still liked to "keep zee love tingling" for West and Annie, as she put it, by giving them a negligee on every special occasion. He loved Aunt Gigi's presents.

"The cards, West," Annie reminded him, half grinning as she guessed where his thoughts were. When he was paying attention, she started. "We got a package with a card for the baby from your parents. They send you their love.''

West could truly smile about that—thanks to Annie. The worry he'd felt about marriage had melted away under Annie's never-wavering love, and he'd come to realize that Matt had been right—they weren't their parents. ''We'll have to call them tomorrow after Zach opens their present.''

''They'll like that.'' Annie pulled the next card free from its envelope and scanned it. ''Whoa, this one's from Jord and Marcia in Germany. Marcia's working part-time on the base and she and Jord are doing fine. Can you believe Teddy just turned three?'' She handed him a snapshot. ''Her letter says they've decided to wait another year so they can really afford to give Teddy a sister or brother and not have to scrimp.''

West gazed at the child in the picture, remembering the square face and the huge eyes. Nothing had changed. But then Zach tried to snatch the photo to chew on, and handing it back to Annie, West laughed. He was wrong. Everything had changed. ''Cute kid,'' he said. ''I'm glad they're waiting, though. That way Teddy will get the best of everything, and they're still young.''

Bending down, West kissed the top of his son's head and then grinned up at his wife. ''But we, on the other hand, are not so young. What do you think about giving Zach a brother or sister? Or is one enough? I don't want you to take on more than you can handle.''

Annie dropped the next card she was opening in

surprise as she gazed at him. They had waited a whole year before she'd conceived Zachery, just so she could prove to West how they belonged together. This time, everything was falling right into place—like a dream come true.

"Not so young?" she asked. "I might have climbed the hill, but I don't think I've fallen down the other side yet. My new partner is working out just fine. Gina is a wonderful baby-sitter. And one is only enough when you're talking about husbands."

"This sounds promising," West said, grinning. "I remember all the negligees we went through working toward Zachery."

"This time we won't have to work at it," she said softly. "This time, we can just plain have fun until June."

"That's when you want to start?" he asked, confused.

"You want to start what?" Matt asked, walking into the kitchen. Gina followed, carrying Wyatt.

"Start taking care of our second baby," Annie said nonchalantly, but her hands had stilled and her eyes were glued to West's face.

His mouth had dropped open, but then Zachery put his whole hand in it, and everyone started laughing.

"At this rate," Gina said, putting her son on his feet, "I'm going to have to call my house a day-care center and get it licensed by the state." She took Zachery out of West's hands. "Hug her, West, before you burst with joy."

West rose and pulled Annie into his arms.

"Merry Christmas, darling," she said. "I should have told you first, but I'm sorry, I couldn't resist."

West slipped his arms around her as little Wyatt spotted what they were doing and pushed their legs closer together, hugging them. Right after him came the spaniel they'd been forced to let Gina adopt from the start when the dog took to her but tried to nip everyone else. West hadn't really minded. He'd had Annie.

The two of them grinned down at their nephew. Turning back to Annie, West found that she was gazing at him with all the love in her eyes he could possibly ever hope for. He returned her look, and he knew he'd been right all along.

Dreams do come true.

* * * * *

MILLS & BOON®

*M*akes
any time
special

Enjoy a romantic novel from
Mills & Boon®

Presents...™ *Enchanted*™ TEMPTATION®

Historical Romance™ ┤MEDICAL ROMANCE™

MILLS & BOON®

Presents...™

MARRIAGE BY DECEPTION *by Sara Craven*

When Ros met Sam Hunter on a blind date, she thought they were the perfect match—if only she hadn't been pretending to be someone else…

A VENGEFUL REUNION *by Catherine George*

Leonie has been working abroad since breaking her engagement to handsome property developer Jonah Savage. Now, he is the first person she meets upon her return! Secretly, Leonie still loves him, but does Jonah share her feelings?

THE ULTIMATE SURRENDER *by Penny Jordan*

When Polly's husband died, his cousin, Marcus Fraser, offered her a home, a job, and himself as surrogate father to her baby. But Polly had to fight her attraction to him, certain that his affection stemmed only from family duty. And then he kissed her…

MISTRESS BY MISTAKE *by Kim Lawrence*

Handsome Drew Cummings had misjudged Eve, believing her to be a calculating seductress in pursuit of his wealthy nephew. So when Drew seemed intent on seducing Eve himself, was he simply protecting his family fortune?

Available from 7th April 2000

MILLS & BOON®

Presents...™

THE SECRET GROOM by *Myrna Mackenzie*

With her promotion at stake unless she marries, Ellen thinks Josh, a lawyer, based in Europe, is the perfect absentee fiancé. Her plan seems foolproof, until the day that Josh turns up to claim his bride…

THE TYCOON'S BRIDE by *Michelle Reid*

Claire was ecstatic when sexy Greek tycoon, Andreas Markopoulou, offered to marry her and adopt her baby sister. But it seemed Andreas would do anything to grant his grandmother's wish to hold her great-grandchild before she died—even if it meant deceiving everyone, including his new bride…

HER BEST MAN by *Christine Scott*

Alex wanted Lindsey to believe that she had a future with him. But to Lindsey, Alex had always been off limits. His good looks and charm ensured his success with other women—but Lindsey's first marriage had taught her never to trust a playboy again…

SUBSTITUTE FIANCÉE by *Lee Wilkinson*

When Blaze Rawdon's fiancée vanishes before their engagement party he ruthlessly coerces Francesca into becoming his stand-in! However, their brief affair three years ago had ended in tears and this time Francesca is determined not to let him touch her heart.

Available from 7th April 2000

MILLS & BOON®

Catherine George

introduces the *Dysart family*

continuing the popular Pennington saga.

The family live at Friar's Wood, a grand
nineteenth–century house and own a
well-respected auction house.

Over the coming months, join the next
generation of Dysarts in their quest to find love
and a partner for life.

A Vengeful Reunion – 7th April 2000

Lorenzo's Reward – 7th August 2000

PLUS more from the Dysarts in 2001

0003/01/LC01

MILLS & BOON®

Three bestselling romances brought back to you by popular demand

Latin Lovers

The Heat of Passion *by Lynne Graham*
Carlo vowed to bring Jessica to her knees,
however much she rejected him. But now she
faced a choice: three months in Carlo's bed, or
her father would go to jail.

The Right Choice *by Catherine George*
When Georgia arrived in Italy to teach English
to little Alessa, she was unprepared for her uncle,
the devastating Luca. Could she resist?

Vengeful Seduction *by Cathy Williams*
Lorenzo wanted revenge. Isobel had betrayed
him once—now she had to pay. But the tears
and pain of sacrifice had been price enough.
Now she wanted to win him back.

*Available at branches of WH Smith, Tesco,
Martins, Borders, Easons, Volume One/James Thin
and most good paperback bookshops*

0002/05

FREE

4 BOOKS
AND A SURPRISE GIFT!

We would like to take this opportunity to thank you for reading this Mills & Boon® book by offering you the chance to take FOUR more specially selected titles from the Presents...™ series absolutely FREE! We're also making this offer to introduce you to the benefits of the Reader Service™—

★ FREE home delivery   ★ FREE gifts and competitions
★ FREE monthly Newsletter   ★ Exclusive Reader Service discounts
★ Books available before they're in the shops

Accepting these FREE books and gift places you under no obligation to buy; you may cancel at any time, even after receiving your free shipment. Simply complete your details below and return the entire page to the address below. *You don't even need a stamp!*

YES! Please send me 4 free Presents... books and a surprise gift. I understand that unless you hear from me, I will receive 6 superb new titles every month for just £2.40 each, postage and packing free. I am under no obligation to purchase any books and may cancel my subscription at any time. The free books and gift will be mine to keep in any case.

POEC

Ms/Mrs/Miss/Mr ....Initials ....
BLOCK CAPITALS PLEASE

Surname ....

Address ....

....

....Postcode ....

Send this whole page to:
UK: FREEPOST CN81, Croydon, CR9 3WZ
EIRE: PO Box 4546, Kilcock, County Kildare (stamp required)

Offer valid in UK and Eire only and not available to current Reader Service subscribers to this series. We reserve the right to refuse an application and applicants must be aged 18 years or over. Only one application per household. Terms and prices subject to change without notice. Offer expires 30th September 2000. As a result of this application, you may receive further offers from Harlequin Mills & Boon Limited and other carefully selected companies. If you would prefer not to share in this opportunity please write to The Data Manager at the address above.

Mills & Boon® is a registered trademark owned by Harlequin Mills & Boon Limited.
Presents...™ is being used as a trademark.